Diana's Dragons
The Awaited

To Myra—
Diana, the dragons,
and I are
glad you're
enjoying the book!
Love,

Dec. 25, 2020

J.R. Schumaker

Diana's Dragons
The Awaited

A Novel

Copyright 2017
J.R. Schumaker
ISBN: 9781549837647

Cover: Linda Griffitts (with contributing artwork by Vicki Heston)

For Noah, Olivia, Joshua-José, and Miguel. Thank you for being you, my four dragon-hearted wonders.

Diana's Dragons
The Awaited

Chapter One

The Awaited

Diana took the back stairs two at a time. Bombs and lasers from her brother's video game chased her out the kitchen door and into the yard. Only where the lawn gave way to wild canyon grass did birdsong begin to replace the ring of explosions in her ears. She ran up the hill through the low brush, zig-zagging as usual to avoid beating a path to her hideaway. She clutched the crystal around her neck. It felt warm, like a breath on her throat. Her heart raced as she lifted the cord, holding the amulet up to the sun. A smoky haze swirled within. Only one thing could awaken the mistcrystal. The dragons: *they were back.*

Her mistcrystal pulled her onward. She rounded the hill and spotted the oak that sheltered the front of her hideaway. The cave faced a gully full of stones and brush that for part of the year also contained a trickling stream. It had been a wet spring, so the rivulet was deep enough to soak Diana's purple high-tops. She avoided the water and the budding branches and then pulled the elucifier, an odd but invaluable object, from one of her many pockets. She shook it gently until it emitted its strange wavelength. She shined the light into the chasm, giving the air inside a ginger-white glow, like an impossible layer of daylight over the dark. The entrance was low, so she had to duck to enter. A grown dragon—the size of a condor—could enter with ease.

Diana's stomach fluttered as fast as her heartbeat. She aimed the beam at the ground as she entered the cavern. It was all she could do to move slowly. She was sure they were here. But were they her dragons? Well, any dragons were welcome. As the splay of light reached the far end of the cave, Diana clamped her hand over her mouth, stifling the urge to cry out. A form was perched on the earthen shelf. She reached for the cave wall to steady herself, felt the chalky rock scratch against her fingertips, and released a sigh she had held since the day her father and Clarin gave her the crystal and disappeared.

Careful not to shine the light near its head, she ran the beam up and down the body. The sleeping dragon was unmistakable now, even in its present slump. The slick blue told her it was a *sea*. It slept with its head in a tuck. A rock shifted under Diana's feet and the creature startled, moving enough to reveal a second creature in the wake of the elucifier's light. A pair! Diana thought her heart would fly out of her chest. Her hand shook so much the elucifier rattled. She advanced slowly and trained the light on the second dragon, a *terra*, golden brown and shining, with its head, too, in a tuck.

Diana sucked in her breath. It could not be a coincidence. A sea and a terra...a *sea* and a *terra*...the words skipped around her mind. Her mistcrystal was fully awake now. It felt like a second, irregular pulse on Diana's throat. Raising the crystal again to her eyes, she watched the amber fog continue its dance, the mist curling like smoke inside the quivering stone. She blinked back tears. Time stopped as she sat with the sleeping dragons and gripped her pendant, everything that mattered contained in its uneven tempo of hope.

Diana shook herself back to the present. *Were these really her dragons? Could this be Clarin and her mate? How could they not be?* She did not dare wake them. Who knew what had driven dragons to sleep during daylight?

Diana checked her watch: 9:00 a.m. There was no way to know when they would awaken.

She backed out of the cave with ginger steps, squinting in the sunlight. Instinctively, she grasped the mistcrystal, feeling it cool a bit as she exited the cave. Pacing between the entrance and a huge boulder, she pulled out her phone and dialed her best friend.

"Hi Diana," Nicki answered the phone quietly. She always managed to sound like she was in a library. "How's it go—?"

Diana broke in before Nicki could finish her sentence. Diana's words buzzed through the phone, "They're back—two of them!"

Nicki gasped, "Oh, my gosh! Which ones? Where are you?"

"At the hideaway—how fast can you get over here?"

"I'll come right now—what do they need? What are they doing?"

"They're asleep. I'm sure they'll be hungry. Oh, and hang by the entrance—what if we *are* strangers? We don't want to scare them."

"OK, no problem. I've got walnuts and bananas. Worms, hmmm...I'll check the compost bin. I'll be there in 15 minutes," Nicki said. Her tone softened. "What about your dad?"

"No, no sign of him," Diana replied, a slight shake in her voice. They fell silent. Diana felt a lump in her throat. She took a step away from the mouth of the cave and continued, her vocal chords giving away her emotion, "But I don't even know what's going on at all yet. I don't even know if it's Clarin and Shay, let alone anything about my dad."

"Yeah, oh, wow. Well..." Nicki's voice trailed off to almost nothing.

"I'm gonna call my mom, then I'm going back inside until they wake up." The best friends hung up.

Diana took a deep breath before calling home. Her mom answered after the three longest rings ever.

"Mom, they're back," Diana gasped in a choked whisper. "The dragons. They made it!"

"Oh, my gosh! I can't believe it. Oh, my...where are they? Are they alright?" Her mom's voice rang out an octave higher than usual.

"They're at the hideaway. They seem fine. They're asleep." Diana bent and peeked into the cave, though it was pointless to try to see through the black.

Her mother sighed and then continued, "And your father—anything?"

"No...no...sorry, Mom," Diana's voice cracked. "No sign."

"OK," her mother was barely audible. Then she perked up, "How many are there? Is it *them*?"

Diana whispered, "Two of them–a *terra* and a *sea*. It has to be...I mean...I bet it's them..." she paused, "but I can't tell yet. And I can't wake them up."

"It must be them," her mother sounded wistful. Silence filled the line. She knew her mom was thinking of Dad. Diana had no words. Then her mother spoke up again, "I'll be right there—"

"Not yet, Mom," Diana answered, "Nicki is on the way with some food. We're OK."

"All right, honey; yes, yes, the two of you are plenty right now. Those poor dragons..." her voice shrank, "what must they have gone through?" She sounded very far away to Diana. Then the familiar focus came back into her mom's voice, "Well, let me know the second you know anything. And check in soon, OK?"

"I will, Mom." Diana was about to hang up, then burst out with the plea, "Mom! Don't tell Brody yet!"

Linda Santos chuckled, "I gave your brother extra time on his video game; if he looks up, I promise, not a word."

Diana double-checked that her phone was on *vibrate* and stooped back into the cave. As she moved toward the back, she felt a tell-tale increase in heat and motion on her throat. Her heart told her this was Clarin. Why else would the mistcrystal enliven so much? After all, it *was* Clarin's very first breath captured in the stone.

Diana swept at some dust on the low stool she kept in the hideaway. She sat watching the dragons for a few minutes. She thought back to the time when her father had first found her in here, alone and crying, after the raven she had tried to nurse to health died. She hadn't even gotten in trouble for running off, though her father insisted on rules and precautions for her cave occupancy from then on. She slid the edge of the elucifier beam along the sea's body. She couldn't get a good look at the dragon from the position in which he slept, and she didn't dare disturb him.

Diana pulled out her phone; Nicki was texting her. She had the food and wanted to know if she should stop at Diana's house and bring a carrier. Diana texted back: "Yes, thanks. Don't let my brother see." What a time to have to be patient. Diana sat motionless. She flicked her wrist to turn off the 'luce, then shook it right back on. The darkness was *too* dark. She held the beam beneath the two dragons and sat for one sixty-second eternity after another. Finally, she saw movement.

It was the terra. Diana could barely contain herself. *Just chill!* she told herself. She leaned past the sleeping sea, gazing at the terra, who was slowly raising her head. The mistcrystal had never been so active. Diana wanted to make sure it was the first thing the dragon saw, in case it was not Clarin, though any terra would feel the presence of the mistcrystal before seeing it. Diana had the kind of butterflies she got on Christmas Eve when she was little, when she had been ninety-nine percent positive what she most wished for was under the tree. The brown dragon opened its eyes. As if it had already seen Diana behind closed lids, their gazes met at once. Diana's heart leapt and her smile felt too wide to be contained in the small space. It was Clarin! Her tawny eyes reached for Diana. Dragons smile with the shape of their eyes, and Diana was drawn into Clarin's, feeling two tiny suns beaming at her. She came close and reached out to touch Clarin's snout. Diana dared not speak, for fear of awakening the *sea*, who, she was sure now, was Clarin's lifelong mate, Shay.

Diana scooted a little closer, kneeling past Shay to touch Clarin's talon. Clarin responded by pressing her snout to Diana's hand. The dragon's touch felt like a summer day condensed into a moment. Diana whispered, "How are you? I missed you so much." Clarin continued to smile, but her thoughts remained silent. Diana followed with the elucifier beam as Clarin bent her head toward a grassy mound between her and her sleeping mate. Diana leaned forward and directed the barest glimmer of light at the grass. Through the nest of brown and green, she caught a tiny glimpse of iridescence. It took only a moment to register: "You laid eggs!" Diana burst out. She pulled the light off the pile; it was a gut reaction—the 'luce couldn't hurt the eggs.

Clarin's whole body sat up taller, her eyes shone. Diana sucked in her breath, then managed to tumble out, "Oh wow, wow..." while daring, with Clarin's approving nods, to brush away a little bit of grass until she saw the radiant shells in pulsating colors: a nest full of eggs of the four dragon natures.

The eggs were a little bigger than golf balls and nearly as round. The shells of all but one kind were extraordinarily hard, their surfaces pearly and luminescent. The nature of the dragonling within was foretold by the color of its shell—*terra:* deep shining gold encased in patches of rich brown, like polished gold ore still surrounded by earth; *sea*: cerulean blue with shimmering, silvery waves; s*un*: deep rose with fiery yellow swirls; and *ghost*: pure, ethereal white. Ghost shells were the thinnest. In the dark, their translucence revealed the glowing outline of the growing hatchling.

A wave of disbelief overtook Diana. It was all hitting her at once. She hunched down on the stool and placed her face in her hands, feeling at any second she would either laugh or cry. The sound of movement on the ledge snapped her out of her reverie, and she looked up to see Shay looking at her, his eyes smiling through his exhaustion. From Clarin's mistcrystal flooded strange, warm feelings; Diana suddenly knew Shay like she'd known him forever. They looked at one another for what seemed like minutes, Diana taking in Shay's deep eyes, feeling as if she'd grown up seeing them her whole life, and at the same time wondering how blue could be so *blue*. She reached for his snout and his warm nuzzle sank into her skin, as the reality that the dragons were home sank into her heart.

Shay turned toward the nest. With great effort, he drew himself up as if to present the eggs. Diana smiled knowingly and told the proud father, "Yes, I've seen. They're beautiful, Shay." Then the dragon father slumped back, giving in to his fatigue.

A text from Nicki buzzed from the phone in Diana's pocket. Nicki was outside the cave. Diana told the dragons, "Nicki's here with some food for you. Be right back." Both dragons nodded and their eyes showed relief. Diana sighed. They would eat. They would be safe. It was all going to be OK. They were home.

Chapter Two

A Dragon, Kin, and The Missive

~Two Years Earlier~

Ten-year-old Diana sprang up in bed. Her hand flew to her neck as if she were reaching for something that was missing, though nothing actually was. Strange light filled the room. She turned, fingers still resting on her throat, to see swirling, colorful light where the wall should be. Diana felt no fear, only a curious pull toward the gently rotating vortex. She stood at the threshold, reaching out to touch the dancing light. As her fingertips met the luminescence, her hand bounced off as if from the surface of a tiny trampoline.

At that moment, a form appeared directly in front of her. She jumped back, leaning on the side of her bed. *What was it? An animal? How was this happening?* A second being emerged within the light: tall, featureless in the kaleidoscopic surroundings, familiar. As her voice crossed the barrier—"Daddy?"—a deep voice spoke back in unison: "Diana!"

Something clacked along the wood floor. Diana turned to see a marble-sized object in front of the portal.

"Honey, quick—pick up the crystal!"

Diana bent to pick up the glassy sphere: a warm, translucent crystal, with gentle dimples of faceting all around encasing a swirling center of glowing amber and smoky fog. The moment she touched it, she heard another voice, not her father's, but inexplicably, just as familiar. Diana spun back toward the portal and trained her gaze on the strange, small figure. The lights played tricks. She saw a crested head, a long snout, and pointed wings. Images from her storybooks flashed through her mind. *Impossible.*

"Diana, I am Clarin," announced a strong, clear, melodic voice *inside Diana's head.*

"Clarin," Diana repeated, feeling as if in a trance. "Who, what?...You look like, like a..."

"Yes, honey. She is. She really is...a dragon," whispered her father.

Again, the song-like voice entered Diana's thoughts, and she thought in reply, *This is your...your* mistcrystal?

Clarin's voice responded at once, *Yes, I give you my mistcrystal. It allows us to communicate without speaking. I ask you to keep it safe*...Something was happening. Darkness tinged the edges of the light.

Diana's father broke in, "Honey, we need you to keep it with you, wear it always, until we can return with the remaining dragons."

"There are more?" Diana nearly shouted.

Yes, said Clarin; her voice already felt natural inside Diana's mind. *My mate, Shay, and I have lost our five young children; they have been taken. They are somewhere in your world.*

Her father broke in, emotion hardening his voice, "—viciously kidnapped from where I found them, Diana, here in..." her father cut himself off.

Darkness overtook more of the portal. Diana reached for Clarin and her father beyond, but was again repelled by the surface of light.

"This portal is one way, one time, Diana," said her father, though he still reached out for his daughter's unreachable hand. "That's why you must do as Clarin asks.

Our dragonkin face grave danger. While you possess my mistcrystal on the other side, you hold the only guide for our return.

Clarin's last few words sounded farther away. The light on the wall had shrunk dramatically. In the diminishing portal, Diana saw her father crouch behind the dragon and heard his voice, now thin and distant. "Diana, it's all going to be OK. Tell Brody I love him. I love you, *Mija*. I miss you all. Tell your mother—"

And the aperture swirled to a close.

Diana sank to the floor with the mistcrystal in her hand, a coldness now emanating from it where the warmth had been. The glittery, smoky center was now still. She held the mistcrystal and her face in her hands. A sudden pulse of warm air startled her. She looked up, hoping to see the portal; in her mind's eye, she saw Clarin and her father stepping through.

The wall of her room had been transformed. Previously a pale violet with animal paw prints painted in darker purple, the entire wall now glowed top to bottom with strange, colorful hieroglyphics, including dragon wings in various orientations.

Diana gaped at the wall. She reached for it with the mistcrystal in her hand. The crystal again came to life and a few of the symbols before her glowed with greater intensity and clarity. Clarin's voice appeared in her mind, saying serenely, *Our Dragonkin family*— Overwhelmed, Diana took a small step back;

immediately the effect was lost as the mistcrystal turned static again. She leaned in and more symbols awakened, as Clarin's voice floated through her, *The four dragon natures...*

Diana ran out of the room and down the hall. Her tightly closed hand pressed the mistcrystal to her chest as she called out, "Mom, Mom, wake up!"

~

"Start with the big symbol; that must be the beginning," Nicki said, pointing to a large, multi-colored picture that looked like four sets of wings extending from a center of tiny, colored dots. "But it's on the wrong side," Diana protested, even as she moved in the suggested direction. "Lots of people read right to left. Or they used to. I think," Nicki said, less sure with every word.

The Dragonkin Missive. Clarin's voice, sounding grand, travelled through Diana's mind as she neared the largest symbol. Diana repeated what she heard to Nicki, who had a notebook and pen in front of her on the bed.

"The Dragon Kin Missive", she wrote at the top of the empty journal, the fast, scratching noises from her pen not matching her unusually neat handwriting.

The girls started at a soft knock on the door. Diana jumped away from the wall, as if she needed to keep its secrets from an intruder. Her mother poked her head in, then said, "We have some visitors."

"Mom!" Diana cried, while Nicki pulled her head back and suspiciously eyed the space where the door opened wider.

"Oh," Diana sighed in relief. Dr. Kimaczynski, their closest neighbor, entered, followed by the local sheriff, Max Gonzales, and his ten-year-old son, Jake. As they cleared the threshold, the adults both swiveled their heads slowly toward the wall of mystery, as if looking for something to leap out at them from around a corner. Linda Santos followed them in, holding fast to the hand of Diana's five-year-old brother, Brody. Brody was trying, to no avail, to pull his mother in the direction of his big sister's new, weird wall.

"Jeez," Jake exclaimed, staring at the wall with wide eyes.

He took a place standing next to Diana, prompting Nicki to use the back of her pen to prod the back of his dark brown leg where it disappeared into dingy athletic socks as she complained, "Hey, you're in my way." He scooted over a few inches. Jake's dad and Dr. Kimaczynski—they all called her Dr. Kim—moved in closer, their eyes floating from one strange symbol to the next. "Go close again!" Nicki shouted, showing a rare hint of giddiness.

Diana leaned toward the largest symbol again and both her mistcrystal and the writing seemed to burn.

"Whoa!" Jake exclaimed and reached for the shining symbol, running his fingers over it. "I thought it would be warm."

"Don't touch the wall," Nicki ordered and received a look from Jake that said, *Excuse me?* But he withdrew his hand.

Dr. Kim said evenly, "Actually, we have no idea how long this will last, do we?"

"That's why we're going to write it all down," Nicki said with quite a bit of authority for her ten years.

"That," Diana again pointed to the largest symbol, "means 'Dragonkin Missive.'"

"We think it's the title," Nicki added.

"Right to left? Interesting," Mrs. Santos said, while looking to the other adults with her eyebrows raised and mouthing, *See?*

"With my own eyes," Sheriff Gonzales said more to himself than to Linda.

"You can say that again," Dr. Kim said, as she walked in an arc to examine the wall, the writing, everything. A retired zoologist, her entire career was based upon observation. "I can't deny what my eyes are showing me."

Linda Santos, a veterinary medicine researcher and animal health blogger, could not disagree.

Diana approached again and recited the words that Clarin's serene tone transmitted, "The four dragon natures are: *ghost, sea, sun, and terra*." Nicki, again scribbling as quickly as possible, bent over the journal in concentration, her straight, jet-black hair falling across her cheek to her chin.

"I might need to sit down," Dr. Kim said after Diana explained that she could actually hear the dragon's voice inside her head. But instead of reaching for the rolling desk chair, the scientist stepped forward. Diana moved along the wall, staying close enough to spark the magical reaction. Various glyphs lit up. Dr. Kim stared and approached the wall, still staring, then shifted her intense gaze to Diana. "What's going on with that one over there?" Dr. Kim asked, reaching toward a roundish symbol of peachy tones with four little dashes extending from one side. The glyph looked like one of Brody's attempts at drawing the sun, but instead of stubby little lines all the way around, the rays were all coming out of the right-hand side.

"What do you mean?" Diana asked, right before Nicki could.

"It looks different from the others," Dr. Kim said. Diana squinted. Everyone else got closer to see. It was true. Rather than remaining flush with the wall like the rest, this one looked like it was painted with puffy fabric paint and filled in.

"When I get close to it, it says 'take the elucifier' and then says a bunch of other stuff. But I don't know what that is. I don't know what it's talking about. I don't know what to do."

"Well," Dr. Kim observed, "since magic seems the order of the day—"at this she shook her head for a moment, like she was trying to jar herself from grogginess—"maybe you should take it more literally." As she tucked a lock of her long, gray hair back behind her ear, she brushed her other hand just above the dragonglyphs. Dr. Kim pulled her hand back, smiling. "Oh, my. Yes, I think you'd better bring that mistcrystal of yours over here!"

Diana complied, looking at her friends and then back at Dr. Kim. She got as close as possible with the mistcrystal, then reached for the elucifier symbol. As her fingers touched the small protrusion, the symbol seemed to grow from the wall; the bit that had seemed just like the other glowing glyphs was actually the tip of something solid. Her mistcrystal took on a gentle orange cast as the object continued to emerge. Diana gasped, tightening her grasp on the palm-sized object. While pulling it free, she heard Clarin's voice announce what it had told Diana a few times before: *The elucifier emits a wavelength that is always safe for dragons and their eggs and does not disturb the full darkness we so crucially require every night.*

Diana stared at her hand.

"It looks like a creamsicle rock," Brody said. Everyone gathered around and stared.

"I wonder how it works?" Nicki asked.

Distracted by the seemingly impossible object, Linda had loosened her hold on Brody's hand. He grabbed the strange stone from his sister and shook it, then dropped it in shock as a bright beam of light hit his face. Still lit, it bounced gracelessly to a stop on Diana's fluffy purple rug. Diana shot her brother a look as she bent down to pick up the precious gift. She shook it again, and the light went out.

"Well, I guess you have yourself an elucifier," said Dr. Kim.

Chapter Three

The Dark Kelling

~The Present~

Casting a longing look at "her" dragons, Diana left the cave, finding Nicki standing next to the entrance with the carrier. She was bouncing on the balls of her feet. The best friends' eyes locked for a moment as they silently shared their secret: the long-awaited return. Diana burst out in a half-shout, half-whisper, "It's Clarin and Shay! And they've got eggs!" Before Nicki could say whatever she'd opened her mouth to say, Diana continued, "It's a big pile— maybe a dozen."

Nicki beamed, "Oh, wow. Wow. I can't believe it. After all this time, they're back *and* they're going to have hatchlings." She rifled around in her pockets and produced a bag of dried fruits and nuts, a banana, and a small container of wriggling earthworms.

"Perfect!" Diana thanked her while putting the fruit into one of her pockets. "You can hang on to those," she said with a shudder of mild disgust, pushing the worms back at Nicki. Quick smiles flickered on their faces,

Diana grabbed Nicki's arm, pulling her to the cave entrance. "Come on! They'll be so happy to see another friendly face."

"I hope so," Nicki half-whispered, as they moved from the bright sunlight into the dark entryway.

"Of course they will. Come on!" Diana tossed back.

Diana led the way. Her light flickered, then regained full magnitude as she neared Clarin. "I wonder if Clarin's drained powers are affecting the 'luce?"

"I guess that's not something I can just look up for us," Nicki joked. Diana felt a renewed excitement with Nicki at her side. With eager eyes, they both searched the light's path. When it landed on the dragons, Nicki sucked in her breath, then sighed, "There they are! They're more beautiful than I imagined."

Both girls stood perfectly still, but for their pumping hearts and heaving lungs. Then Nicki knelt on the cave floor and extended a hand and tentative grin to each dragon. Nicki closed her fingers on each of the dragon's snouts, looking over to Diana and observing, "So warm...wow." As the dragons nuzzled into her palm, she stroked them gently.

"Oh, it is so good to meet you. I always believed, but seeing is, well, kind of unbelievable." Nicki sounded breathless. Diana nudged her friend after a few moments, and Nicki exclaimed, "Oh, and I bet you're hungry!"

The dragons looked on expectantly as Nicki pulled out the worms. Diana marveled at how majestic the dragons looked, even with their eyes trained on the coming meal. Nicki held out a palm to each dragon while displaying none of the squeamishness Diana showed just in watching.

"Protein first. You look so worn out," Nicki said in her usual scientist's voice. Diana held the elucifier over everyone's head so that in the dark she could just make out two black tongues darting toward Nicki's open palm, reeling in three or four of the wrigglers at a time.

"That tickles," Nicki said as she brushed her hands off on her crisply pressed pants before holding out the next serving. The rest of the worms were gone in mere seconds, followed by the fruit, which Diana offered.

As soon as their food was consumed, the dragons seemed to shrink, heads tilted toward the eggs, wings drooping.

Concern bit at Diana's elation. "I know nesting has to take it out of them, but they look like they've been through a lot more," she whispered to Nicki.

"So true. What else can we do for them?"

Diana leaned on the wall of the cave, hands deep in her khaki pockets, her eyes slits as she stared at the dragons, as if she could see what they'd been through just by squinting at them.

Without warning, Diana's eyes popped open and she jumped to attention, her face filled with alarm. "Oh no!" Diana cried. "What's that?!"

"What's wrong? What's *what?*!" Nicki shouted, bewildered.

Clarin and Shay sprang to their feet, Clarin arching her body over the eggs like a shield against something about to rain down from the sky. Diana's body shook; her hand flew to her mistcrystal.

Shay looked toward the mouth of the cave, eyes wide, his wings open as far as the small space allowed. The mistcrystal was emitting a sound only dragons could hear—a sound every dragon dreaded. Though Diana could not hear the unearthly alert, she instinctively recognized the erratic thrum as evil. *What was happening?*

The dark kelling.

Diana burst out, "What? How?—" She could hear Clarin—*how was it possible?* Discord and angst replaced the calm, melodious dragon voice Diana remembered from when they first met.

Clarin's thoughts ripped through Diana's mind: *The dark kelling—the dreaded effect produced when a mistcrystal and a desecrated shiftcrystal found their way near each other—was upon them.* Shiftcrystals, by dragonkin sanctity, lay only in baby dragons' graves.

From the moment it struck, Diana and the dragons were swept into its effect: they began to *speed up through time.* Soon, they would be absorbed into the kelling dimension, moving so quickly they would be invisible to the others. The eggs would remain helpless and vulnerable.

Clarin's voice again racked Diana's mind: *The dark kelling will kill the eggs.* Diana shuddered.

"The dark kelling...the dark kelling..." Diana repeated the phrase like a nefarious hypnotist, staring at Nicki. Nicki grabbed her by the shoulders and Diana's confused expression turned to one of horror. Nicki shook her and Diana snapped back to attention. "We've got to get the eggs out of here!" Diana shouted, then seemed to shake herself. "No, *I've* got to get away from them! They'll crack!"

Her last words were now reaching Nicki's ears at an unnaturally high pitch. It was happening fast. Diana felt a sudden tug at her back pocket. She spun around to see her raggedy safari hat in Nicki's slow-moving hands. "Right!" she screeched, and pulled a bandana from one of her many pockets, tossing it onto the hat. Clarin had pulled back from her hover over the eggs, giving Nicki access to the nest.

"Complete cover!" Diana shouted, already moving away but desperate to be understood as she watched Nicki move before her in slow-motion, lining the hat with the bandana. Diana steadied her voice and lowered it, speaking in what sounded to her ears like a bizarre imitation of her droning Math teacher. Her stomach churned. "You've gotta keep them safe—" The trembling of the mistcrystal strengthened. *Was the shiftcrystal getting closer?*

Clarin and Shay led the way to the mouth of the cave; their exhaustion had evaporated under the effects of the dark kelling. Nicki's face contorted with worry, but she nodded. "I'll call your mom. Don't worry—"

"Get them to Dr. Kim's—" Diana could not tell whether Nicki had understood, though her mouth was open as if to reply.

Nicki's voice was low, too slow for Diana's ears. Everyone and everything apart from Diana and the dragons was grinding to a halt.

The vibrations at Diana's neck surged in a frenzy just as they lost sight of Nicki and the eggs. In that second, they heard it: the horrifying crack followed by the tell-tale moan that emanates from a dying dragon egg. Though the dragons' ears were filled with the pervasive alarm, the cleaving of their unborn crashed through their consciousnesses. Every heart and stomach in the cave lurched in sickness and grief. Diana and the dragons tore, heartbroken, from the cave.

Once outside, Diana stumbled as her eyes adjusted to the blinding sunlight. She nearly slammed into Clarin a few feet from the entrance. The dragon had stabbed her claws straight down into the ground. She pulled up two clumps of dry earth and held them together before her. As she slowly separated her talons, the soil between them seemed to dissolve, yet entangle. It stretched like spiderweb suspended in a gritty, glittery haze, and then spun into a threadless, shimmering cloth. As Clarin continued to pull her claws apart, the magical textile expanded within her wingspan. In seconds, she was holding a pair of gossamer wings the color of the earth. The markings exactly matched Clarin's. This was Diana's *elementor*.

Diana bowed beneath the apparatus, allowing it to conform to her back and arms. It became part of her, no different than her own limbs and skin. *Just let go and feel my lead*, Clarin instructed. *You will fly as surely as I do.* Diana felt herself give in to Clarin's impulses. Her new wings, her body, responded to wordlessly synchronized movements, as automatic as raising her feet to walk. The wings lifted her in tandem with the dragon, the weight of her human limbs somehow disappearing. A carefree sense filled her like never before as she lost the division between Clarin's impulses and her first flight.

The newly found bliss was quickly replaced by urgency and the bitter drive she shared with Clarin and Shay to prevent more loss. They fled, Diana flying between the two dragons, all of them desperate to put as much distance as possible between themselves and the defenseless eggs.

Nicki, having called Diana's mother as promised, stood with her face to the cave entrance, the eggs to her left. She aimed the elucifier—Diana had dropped it through either panic or quick thinking—toward the entrance so the sunlight from outside nearly met the limit of the beam. She remained at her post like the Guardian of the Holy Grail until finally Diana's mother appeared at the mouth of the cave. Linda Santos rushed to the vigilant gatekeeper to see on her face a story of pain. She listened to everything, finally muttering, "Oh, dear God. It sounds so sinister: the dark kelling..."

Diana's mother regarded the nest, all the anticipated delight at the dragons' return having dissipated into fear and concern. Nicki stood by her, lighting the way with the elucifier. Mrs. Santos put an arm around Nicki's shoulder.

"Diana was just able to say a few words before she, well, disappeared," Nicki all but whispered. "They just started to speed up until I couldn't see or hear them." Nicki's shoulders drooped, and her voice quavered, "She said to guard the eggs. We have to keep them safe."

"Then they are already far away." Linda Santos forced calmness into her words, "They'll be fine, and they'll figure this out."

"Diana wants us to take the eggs to Dr. Kim's," Nicki said.

"Good idea. This hideaway is no longer safe. Our house could be next." Diana's mother said quietly, "I can't believe this is happening. They just got here."

Nicki stood taller. "But at least they're home." Then she sank back into a slump, her eyes cast toward the ground. "We lost an egg."

Mrs. Santos gave Nicki a soft, sad look, then let out a sigh. "Let's get going. How're we transporting the eggs?"

Nicki produced Diana's hat and purple bandana.

The tiniest smile pulled at Linda's lips. "Well, some things we can always count on." She stroked the brim of the hat. Mrs. Santos held the elucifier while Nicki alternately placed soft grass and the precious cargo into the mobile nest. She came to the broken egg, which felt frozen. Nicki hesitated.

"Here, let me," Mrs. Santos intervened. She took a tissue from her pocket and swaddled the broken shell, then placed it in her pocket. "So cold."

Nicki tapped the pile with the lightest of touches to be sure the eggs were settled and well-cushioned. She tied the bandana so it was snug, but not too tight.

They looked down at the bundle. "Eleven," Nicki said.

"And their first five children are still missing," Mrs. Santos added. Gloom reigned over the dark hideaway, the glow from the self-radiating eggs having been the only relief. The silence seemed to seep into the black walls. Diana's mother gripped the clutch of eggs with both hands. Nicki lit their path to the front, each of them moving as if their sneakers on the packed ground could shatter the shells.

The sun beat on the entrance to the cave. Nicki turned. "It's too bright. We should cover them better," she said.

"Good idea."

Nicki ran back and began brushing together the rest of the grass from the original nest. As her hand grazed the ledge, she heard a soft grating sound. She swept at the grass and felt a small, solid object. Sliding it across the shelf and into her hand in one fast motion, she gripped it, then slipped it into her pocket. She ran back to Mrs. Santos and emptied the handfuls of grass onto the already odd-looking nest.

They made their way slowly through the bramble, stepping as carefully as if through a minefield. They reached the car and after Nicki belted herself in, Mrs. Santos placed the eggs in her lap. Nicki wanted to check for texts, a form of communication she expected they could still depend upon through the gap in speed, but she didn't dare loosen her grip on the eggs. "Diana and the dragons..." Nicki gulped, "...they have to be OK."

"Yes, they have to be," Linda Santos answered in that voice mothers use to assure others and reassure themselves. "They just have to be." She started the engine of the old hatchback and headed straight for Dr. Kim's.

Chapter Four

The Break-in at Illsworth's

The three navigated like a flock of geese, changing direction together, tracking the source of the dark kelling. At the other end of the ghastly vibration would be the shiftcrystal and their adversary. The villain would be unaware of their presence, as the dark kelling sparked the superspeed—the kelling dimension—only for dragons and now, the bearer of a mistcrystal.

The trio continued to travel at their personal hyperspeed. Clarin and Shay were better than Diana at following the intensity of the dark kelling because the haunting sound pulsed directly through their hearts. They alighted on an outcropping of boulders. They had covered a lot of ground. "Should the eggs be out of range by now?" Diana asked, though the dragons must have known so or they would not have stopped.

Diana saw a dark gray lizard on a rock next to them. She knew from Dr. Kim that it was a western fence lizard. At least twice a week,

Diana jumped and shrieked at one of the tiny creatures scuttling along a sidewalk. As much as she loved animals, she could never quite deal with the kinds that darted around on the ground near her feet. Now, as it appeared to glide, snail-like, rather than skitter across the chalky boulder, it seemed silly to even think of being afraid of it.

Diana pointed east and the dragons nodded. They took off again. She knew the area like the back of her hand. They crossed the north fork of the meager creek and followed the bank. The alternating shade and pinpricks of sun through the canopy of pepper and oak trees flashed like reverse lightning above them. A mile or so ahead of them lay the sprawling estate of Marcurius Illsworth.

"Furious Marcurius," the adults who had dealings with him had named him; he was "Icky Illsworth" to Diana's seven-year-old brother and the other little kids in Pasqual Valley. Even the most rebellious didn't cross him or his property line. A shiver ran down Diana's spine. They came to a landing just over the hill, perching atop another huge boulder outcropping. They all gazed in the direction of Illsworth's grounds. An avocado grove obscured the dark stone of the gigantic house.

"Illsworth," Diana said, speaking aloud to include Shay. She bestowed a look of gloom on her companions. "If anyone would be up to something terrible, it's him."

Aching sadness eclipsed Diana's other feelings, and then: dread. She cried out, "Illsworth probably knows something about Dad!" This realization, coupled with viewing the horrid man's sprawling property, pushed the powerlessness Diana had coped with for the past two years into her heart all at once.

He couldn't just be a jerk, Diana thought to Clarin, anger and frustration rising inside her, *he had to do something evil to you, to some poor dragon baby's grave; to your babies...*

Diana trailed off as guilt crept through her. *I'm sorry. I'm so sorry about your baby.* The wrenching sound they had heard as the egg was destroyed flooded her.

Clarin returned no thoughts, but she couldn't mask the mournful ache, nor the anguished look she exchanged with her mate. Clarin and Shay paused for a few moments, eyes locked. They looked to be sharing one slow, labored breath.

When Clarin again shared her thoughts with Diana, she assured her: *We follow the dark kelling*. Clarin, still looking at Shay, nodded her head and replied in thought, *Yes, it is strange that the dark kelling is nearly as strong here as it was when it began. It must be Illsworth who somehow stole a shiftcrystal. But by what dark means?*

Diana listened, puzzled, as Clarin explained: *A baby dragon's shiftcrystal contains dreadful potential if pillaged from its sanctified ground. Only a shiftcrystal disturbed in such a way could set off the warning of the dark kelling.*

Diana clenched her fists, felt her heart harden and her pulse start to race again.

Breathe, child, Clarin thought, in a whisper that seemed to fill Diana's lungs with sweet, still air.

The mother dragon stood tall. As a terra, her brown scales could sometimes seem duller than those of the other natures, but in the dappled sunlight, their subtle gloss seemed to match the growing gleam in her eye. Any unease in her expression dissolved, replaced by a look of granite, beautiful and unbreakable. The flecks in her eyes glinted like actual gold, highlighting the spatter of amber scales that fanned out from the center of her face to the edges of the spiny crests on her cheeks.

Diana tried to absorb Clarin's confidence. She tilted her face toward the rays of sun that fell through the palms, giving her olive skin darker stripes. Her brown hair shone, and her nearly black eyes drew in extra light. She took in the incandescent blue of Shay's scales. A silvery blue-green flourish ran from his chest to his brow. It matched the color of his eyes so closely his irises appeared only as an oceanic shimmer surrounding fathomless pupils. He drew himself up. The three, in a collective, steadfast stance, took off from their lookout point and descended into Illsworth's dusky world.

Clarin led them to a stop once more, with just the avocado grove and fence between them and the grounds.

Clarin thought, *We will set off the alarms, but no one can reach us.* Diana and Shay nodded in unison, but Clarin raised her talon and shrugged, looking like a human raising her index finger to say, "Just one thing..."

"Right," Diana jumped in, reading her concerns. Clarin nodded. Diana continued, "I can't touch a stolen shiftcrystal while wearing the mistcrystal. And if I take it off, I fall out of the kelling dimension—" her hand shot up to her neck, "...and I could lose the mistcrystal."

Both dragons looked at Diana with expectation. If dragons had eyebrows, she imagined they would each be raising one at her.

Clarin's clear voice instructed her, *If you touch the shiftcrystal while wearing the mistcrystal, the dark kelling will invade your mind and do...do we know not what, possibly terrible injury*—the dragons' imaginary eyebrows shot up further—*or worse.*

Diana returned a look of compliance and said with deference, "I know. Yes, I know. Thank you. I won't be forgetting."

Clarin and Shay nodded and their eyes relaxed.

Clarin wasn't finished. *If he possesses the desecrated shiftcrystal, Illsworth may wield magic that the dragonkin ourselves recall only in legends.* Diana gulped as Clarin continued, *It is not unreasonable to suspect he is involved with the disappearance of our children—"*

Diana was shaken to hear unsteadiness in Clarin as the dragon continued, *but I cannot feel their presence, nor can Shay.* Her mate remained stoic. But Diana could feel the weight, the worry, as the names of their lost children drifted through Clarin's mind: *Ayan, Merac, Tynan, Tethys, Gryn*...Diana sighed as tears threatened to form. It was the first time

Diana had sensed anything anchorless in the dragon matriarch.

Diana never felt so determined. "We'll find them," she swallowed and then added in a near whisper, "and I hope we find something out about my dad." She looked at her friends, whose faces revealed their sympathy.

Clarin's thoughts suddenly seemed rushed, but crystal clear, *I'm sorry I know so precious little. Your father disappeared—I don't know how— almost the moment the portal through which we came to you closed. He was able to communicate with us once, for an instant, before we returned. Again, I don't know how he managed it...*

Diana cut in a little too loudly, "Then he must have some power, wherever he is..." She felt new resolve. "OK, so we'll get in and find the shiftcrystal, then get out," she said, for no reason but to steel herself further.

Shay drew Diana's attention to him with a quick flap of his wings, while Clarin simultaneously conveyed in thought, *Shay will take it. He will guard it until we can recommit it to the earth.*

Someplace safe, Diana thought.

Someplace unseen, Clarin replied.

Diana led the way to the east side of Illsworth's expansive property. They flew just above the fence of close-set, black bars topped by foot-long iron spikes.

Diana watched her shadow falling over the fence, its sharp points at odd angles. The fence looked like something from medieval times. It was all so *ill*. Even though he had the whole place wired with alarms, the fence sent the message: *You, your pet, your dragon, or anything remotely kind and decent: keep out!* Illsworth seemed to have a beef with all fellow creatures; those with magical powers probably threatened him to the brink.

They reached the side gate. Tall, skeletal eucalyptus trees were doing all they could to defend the back of the house against sunshine. The grounds were dotted with messy bottle brush trees and stout date palms. The rest of the dense landscaping was filled in by prickly desert foliage. It was complete coincidence that Illsworth's plants were eco-friendly, requiring little water. Illsworth was friendly to nothing and no one. It was the spikes, thorns, and barbs emerging from the yuccas, jumping cactus, and thistle sage that attracted Illsworth.

The house itself was a huge one-story "ranch," she thought her mother called it.

While all the other houses around the valley were covered in California stucco—light and practical, if a little boring—Illsworth's house was constructed of dark, rough stone blocks. Diana's father had talked about watching the house being built when he was a little kid, when there was nothing else around in the valley.

Jeff Santos and his friends used to play in the fields, looking for coyote tracks or other evidence of the wildlife's night before. When the foreign men and materials arrived to build Illsworth's manor, it looked like an ancient European castle was going up, until the modern smoke-belching yellow machines arrived to do their work. No one from Pasqual Valley worked on the construction. All the workers stayed on the property, and everything they needed was brought in. The delivery people dealt only with Illsworth and left the pallets and supplies at the end of the drive for his workers to haul.

The entire valley was consumed with curiosity. There were even a few break-in attempts by teenagers on a dare. Illsworth's security was impenetrable. Jeff and the other younger boys learned to keep their distance, as the mysterious new owner sometimes stood vigil at the edge of the construction site. When the boys got too close one day, he turned his disturbing visage toward them. With a brandish of his walking stick and a glare from his mismatched eyes, he ran them off via chills down their spines. None of his later attack dogs or alarms would be more effective deterrents.

"Rrrrrrrrrrr." A low, slow growl drew their eyes to the walk where it started to wrap around the house. There lay two giant black dogs, chins hovering inches above the cement.

"Oh, his guard dogs, poor things." Diana had heard stories about the brutal tactics Illsworth used to train his dogs. She didn't know how much of it was true, but she was sure that a "pet" here was not really treated like a pet.

"Good dogs!" Diana called, sure that the ultra-speed soprano of her voice would somehow register in the dogs' brains. Diana and the dragons gave the snail-paced pooches sympathetic glances. The dogs were barely getting to their feet, yearning to progress toward what they could not see from their normal positions in time.

Diana and the dragons landed on the back patio. Diana tried the back door; it was locked, of course. She rattled it. The alarms tripped. In the ears of the super-speeders it sounded like a drawn-out bang on the world's largest gong.

They circled the house and came upon the front door, which stood open just a crack. Inside, a thuggish type in khaki pants and a green shirt stood with his hand on the knob. He had one eyebrow arched and a hard line to his mouth. They pulled the door from his grip and ducked under his arm. He would never understand what had happened. They had just enough room to slip by. Diana's elementor fell to repose down her back, a gauzy cape too light to feel on her body, but its ever-readiness present in her mind. She zipped through the doorway with the dragons on her heels.

"Let's hope it all goes this smoothly," she said, leading the way into the house. Two more guard dogs stood by the door. Their heads were cocked at a deliberate angle, ears up. Diana petted them, although she knew her touch would barely be felt. "Funny to see their expressions in slow-motion, isn't it?" It was a sloppy, happy look, not the look elicited by a typical trespasser. They left the dogs, their black noses quizzically angling toward the origin of the phantom affection.

Illsworth's foyer was a nightmare. In fact, it was very close to real nightmares Diana had dreamed about this place. If her dad had ever made it inside, he would have seen that his boyhood impression of the dark castle held true: dark stone walls inside. *Who had stone walls inside?* It was the perfect setting for a horror film. Or a horror reality. The floors were also stone, also dark. The place was a museum of dark.

Diana shivered. "It's worse than I imagined," she said.

We're closer to the shiftcrystal, of that I'm certain, Clarin answered, also adding a heightened sense of protection, which Diana felt without words. The dragons moved closer to her.

The muted stone of the manor created an atmosphere of complete cheerlessness, and the *décor* sunk the place into downright depression. The halls and walls were lined, floor to ceiling, with the stuffed bodies and heads of hunted animals: big game trophies, dozens upon dozens of them. *Trophies*, thought Diana. Her chills turned to nausea.

To her right stood a stuffed, flaxen-colored mountain lion. It was permanently poised as if descending the fake hillside upon which it was mounted, surrounded by dried grass and eucalyptus stems, its mouth open. The teeth of the cat were bared but the expression was no more ferocious than that of Diana's cat, Curly, when she stared through a window at a bird. Diana reached out instinctively to touch the thick fur. It was soft. She petted the side of the paralyzed feline, willing her touch to reanimate it. She wanted to set it free in the canyon and watch it run up the hill, away from Illsworth, away from death, back to its life.

In the center of the foyer was an enormous bearskin rug. She thought the fleeting and ridiculous question, *Why do they call it bearskin? It's so furry.* It was such a loss, all that natural luxury, now only a coat for Illsworth's cold floor. The bear's arms were outstretched in a pose of supplication, black claws pointlessly extended. *And his poor head is still attached,* Diana whispered to herself. She saw that the tip of one ear was broken off. She frowned at the indignity of it as they all stepped reverently around the disheartening hide.

Deer, elk, and other antlered prey of every ilk—Dr. Kim would know their names—looked down on them from perfectly crafted mountings. Three and four rows of the poor things peered down through glassy eyes. Standing amidst all the stuffed death, Diana's next sight brought an extra wave of sickness, which then gave way to sadness. There, placed in prime positions above the massive fireplace, were four empty mountings bearing brass plates. Each was engraved with the identity of Illsworth's next intended conquests: *Terra, Sea, Sun, Ghost.*

Diana clenched her fists, a deep flush rising to her neck and face. Her legs went rigid and her knees locked. She felt the dungeon around her begin to spin. She clutched her stomach, then heard Clarin's reassurance in her thoughts—firm, calm, grounding: *Never mind. It means nothing.* Clarin and Shay stood at each of her sides. *In fact, it may be a good sign that our children are still alive.* Diana's churning stomach and swirling anger began to settle. A terra's reassurance was an elixir for any anxiety.

The dragons came in closer to her, almost in a huddle. They were steady, unperturbed. She felt the warmth emanating through their scales. Two years of missing her father and wondering about these wondrous creatures pervaded her mind. *Her father.* She thought about the last time she had seen him, and before that, how it had felt when he hugged her before he went away for work. It was only supposed to be a month. *Two years.* A sigh welled up inside her. With the dragons close by her side, she released the memories—for now.

Clarin slipped down a hall, silent but for her talons tapping on the cold, unforgiving marble. Diana's crystal vibrated more frenetically. The thrum of the dark kelling was strong, but she had become accustomed to the feeling on her neck. Shay followed Clarin, with Diana close behind. "The shiftcrystal—it's really close, isn't it?" Diana asked just to hear her own voice, which she hoped didn't sound as unsteady as it felt. Clarin stopped at one of the huge wooden doors lining the wide, darkly paneled hallway.

Diana stepped in front of the dragons, reaching for the ornate silver doorknob, but Clarin stretched out a wing to block her. *Terras* were known for incredible hearing. When possessing full powers —as they seemed to in the kelling dimension, even while expecting hatchlings—this keen sense was accompanied by the terra's ability to detect emotion. Diana was not about to second-guess her.

"It's in here, then...the shiftcrystal," Diana stated with a dry gulp. A look of warning overtook Clarin's features. Diana reached for the door again, opening it just a few inches. "What a surprise. Dark and dim in there, too."

Shay stepped forward. *Seas* had exceptional vision, including unparalleled night vision. The magical extension of this allowed them to see through fog, steam, cloudy water—all things misty or murky. He peeked inside and jutted one pointed shoulder forward, indicating that the other two follow. He pushed into the room with Clarin and Diana close behind.

All three stood dumbstruck. It was impossible. Illsworth was standing right there, but he was *moving*. He stood in front of the tall windows, dissected by a yellow edge of light attempting to penetrate the heavy drapes. The sharp slivers of sun bounced off a large ring on his finger: a cage-like silver setting holding a gleaming, blood-red gem with a jagged bolt of black through the center: the shiftcrystal.

How could this be? Here was Illsworth, wearing what could only be an unthinkably acquired shiftcrystal, his hand halfway to his belt, moving at an unnaturally slow, but visible, pace. He gave no indication of awareness of their presence.

Marcurius Illsworth suffered from pale, white skin and oily, brutally cropped gray hair. His square-ish head sat atop a thick neck and tall, yet stocky, frame. He was nearly seventy, though he was remarkably unlined for his age.

He had a wide face with tiny red capillaries showing through a pallid hide. Perched on his ample, crooked nose were thick glasses, the square metal frames belonging to a past decade. He had one beady, milky gray-blue eye and one eye of glass, also some shade of gray. An optometry technician had worked hard to create a mirror image of his real eye, but this was not quite achieved; so it was not the glass eye itself that was terribly grotesque, but the unnatural, mismatched effect.

Illsworth dressed in plain, dull work shirts, sagging jeans, and gray boots that everyone suspected were made of some poor, endangered pelt. His belt, worn to colorlessness, was incongruent with its over-polished silver buckle adorned with a sharp, black claw. On his right index finger he wore the macabre ring. As far as Diana and the dragons knew it was the only shiftcrystal possessed by anyone, human or dragon, outside a burial ground.

Diana had expected to feel fear and powerlessness upon finding anything here—Illsworth, the shiftcrystal, clues about the dragons or her father—especially in his lair. But at the sight of him in the slowed dimension, two years of pent-up emotion surged to the surface. Her jaw and fists clenched, her breath came in labored bursts of fury. Clarin stepped in front of Diana before she could do something impulsive.

Diana wanted to shake Illsworth, to demand that he hear her, force him to tell her anything he knew about her father, to return the shiftcrystal to whatever burial site he had ripped it from, and to demand that he not be Icky Illsworth or Furious Marcurius, but a decent human being.

Clarin's soft thoughts brought Diana back down. A wave of shame rode through her. The dark kelling must be excruciating for the dragons, now that they were so close to the shiftcrystal. For Diana, the pulse in the mistcrystal felt like bass drum beats reverberating along her clavicle.

"Are you OK?" Diana directed her thoughts to both of them, though only Clarin could hear her. She sensed the dragon's pain caused by the dark kelling, but they just looked at Diana, their faces inscrutable.

How is he able to move so quickly that we can observe it from the kelling dimension? Clarin thought. *It should be impossible.*

53

Shay took a deliberate step toward the villain, prepared to somehow pluck the shiftcrystal from its setting.

Diana, on pins and needles, approached Illsworth as closely as she dared. *He looks pretty mad*, she thought. A small device resembling a car key remote was clipped to Illsworth's belt and lay at the end of his slowly extending grasp. "Look!" Diana cried aloud, just as she heard Clarin's voice, *Look over here—now*. Clarin had broken off of their study of Illsworth to check the rest of the room. Diana felt Shay's thumb talon pressing on her shoulder. He pointed his other wing back toward the door and Clarin, and he seemed to freeze. Diana swallowed and turned. She jumped toward Shay, her hand reaching for the slightly stabbing wing and grabbing on.

On either side of the door through which they had just passed stood a large bird of prey, about three feet tall with scraggly, greasy-looking black feathers. The two appeared to be standing watch. *Vultures*.

Diana and Shay rushed to Clarin's side. They studied the imposing birds, which stood just an inch or two shorter than the dragons. Diana had never seen a vulture close up, though she saw them every day when the animal preserve near her house fed its resident birds, and hundreds of the black scavengers occupied the trees, waiting for their chance to steal a meal from the captives.

Diana shivered at the sight of sparse feathers poking out of raw red pores. Their heads looked like tomatoes, with inside-out, spongy crimson skin clinging all the way down their gaunt faces. The smooth, bone-colored beaks were the only part of their appearance that was not disconcerting. Each bird had a black, rectangular object hanging around its neck.

Shay stepped closer to the vulture on the right, peering at the black box. Diana followed, then zipped back to Illsworth, whose hand was just landing on the device hanging from his belt. All of the objects bore the same symbol: the ouroboros, a dragon circled around on itself, looking as if it swallowed its own tail. For someone endowed with super-speed, Diana certainly felt a slow prickling of fear creeping over her.

Danger pushed into Diana's and the dragons' brains at the same moment. This scene was very wrong. *Get out!* they thought in unison, Diana shouting it out instinctively while bolting with Shay and Clarin toward the door. They ran out of the house, the dragons breaking into flight from the stone porch, hanging in the air, hovering over Diana, who would never make it into flight fast enough to clear the fence.

Diana was at the gate when it happened, the dragons just above her. Vultures flew out from over the house; they flew at Diana and the dragons at *kelling dimension speed*.

"The kelling dimension is gone!" she shouted. But from the corner of her eye she could see the dogs making the same sluggish progress as before. Her panicked feet tried to keep up with her thoughts. It didn't make any sense. *How were the vultures flying at full speed?* As Diana grasped the gate handle, Clarin and Shay treaded air, their eyes riveted on the approaching attackers. They turned on the vultures, claws gleaming in the late morning sun.

Diana was through the iron door. Over the metallic slam, she heard loud screeches from both dragons. Vultures torpedoed toward Diana—six of them. Diana ran toward the trees just in front of her, her elementor billowing at her back. She dared not fly into the thick trees; she dared not look back. The dragons flew behind her, turning to face the guard raptors, extending their leathery wings in an effort to intimidate the vultures. Illsworth's black sentinels flapped their wings in fury and extended their talons forward in unnatural looking postures of threat.

Clarin and Shay each faced a vulture, brandishing their chiseled appendages—they had the advantage of clawed feet *and* clawed wings. They swiped at the closest vultures, then whirled in the air to fend off the next bird. The quickness of the dragons and the sharp precision of their strikes sent the vultures into a frenzy of defense that left them wobbling in the air.

Too stubborn to give up, or driven by whatever hold Illsworth had over them, the haggard birds regained their bearings and flew at the dragons all at once. Even with the dragons' lightning reflexes, six huge birds would do some damage. Diana heard Clarin cry out woefully, "I'm sorry, my fellows. You leave us no choice." With that, she unleashed a warning flare of golden firebreath, singeing the feathers of the nearest vulture. Two approaching raptors flew up and away at the sight of the fire. But still, half of the vultures stabbed at the dragons' backs. Shay spun and dove, releasing a blue-white cascade of flame that repelled the rear onslaught.

Diana scrambled to the lowest branch of the first climbable tree and watched in horror, her nose filled with the stench of burning feathers. The vultures split off and two of them headed toward Diana. The others flew to surround the dragons. Clarin and Shay evaded the approach and positioned themselves in the air between the birds and Diana, breathing shields of fire in front of them.

"Look out!" she cried as one of the vultures tore in from the side and slammed into Clarin. Clarin had moved just in time to avoid a hard hit, and the vulture piled into the tree, shaking Diana's branch so that she started to slip.

Diana grabbed onto the trunk. Her back was exposed and the sounds of the fight sent chills through her body. She heard Shay's bellow; she heard wings flapping and feathers chafing, felt the heated air. She maneuvered along the branch trying to free her hands again. Suddenly, there was only silence and stillness.

In an instant, the barrage had come to a halt. Like battered remote-control toys, all six vultures disengaged and flew off. Diana lost her hold on the branch and slipped to the ground with a thump. She turned her head to see the vultures flying toward the house. Diana exhaled. She and the dragons were left in a vacuum of quiet.

Clarin and Shay flew to Diana and landed next to her. Diana gave her friends a look of relief that was not returned. Their eyes were fixed on the house. Diana followed their sight lines. Illsworth stood by the fence, his hand on the black box attached to his belt like a corrupt lawman's hand twitching on his holster.

It was clear that Illsworth had called off the birds. But how had he reached the yard so fast? He should not have gotten a tenth of the way across the floor of his creepy parlor in the time that had elapsed. He glared at them as they sat beneath the quaking leaves, his face a mix of rage and satisfaction.

"What in the world is going on?" Diana queried aloud. The dragons remained fixed on Illsworth. He aimed a crooked finger in their direction. His gestures were in slow-motion and deliberate, cartoonish. "He's not in the kelling dimension with us, is he?" The dragons shook their heads. They had no idea how he had managed what he had with the vultures. They had no idea how he could see them or move in this strange in-between speed. They had no idea what the symbol on the sinister devices meant. They knew one thing now: Illsworth had learned some terrible tricks. One dragonling had already lost its life. They had to find out what he was up to before he caused more   pain.

Chapter Five

A New Nest

Illsworth continued to look toward the pepper tree for a few of the longest minutes of Diana's life. Then he turned away with his improbable alacrity and stepped toward the house. The vultures had flown into the same openings from which they had appeared. Diana could just make out what looked like a giant skylight closing on the roof. She could not see the entire rooftop from her vantage point, so it appeared as if some of the vultures were just sucked into the house.

I wonder how many are in there, Diana thought, wariness sticking to each word. "Let's get out of here," Diana continued. They moved away from Illsworth's manor, heading for Dr. Kim's.

Diana obeyed Clarin's warning to stay on foot: *If the kelling dimension fails, my power to elevate you will also fail.* The elementor draped behind Diana, as airy as cobwebs. If not called upon again soon, it would dissolve into even airier particles of the elements from which it was sown.

The dragons flew low. They would face unbelievable exhaustion as soon as the kelling dimension was lost. They outpaced some deer; and, as they crossed the creek, the flight of nearby birds appeared only slightly slower. The kelling dimension was diminishing rapidly the farther they removed themselves from Illsworth and his mysterious manipulations with the shiftcrystal.

Clarin and Shay flew inches above the earth. *Let us walk now*, suggested Clarin. But the very next moment, the dimension ceased, and the two dragons tumbled awkwardly to the ground. They sank into the brush, looking like strange, shiny rock piles poking through the sage. Diana ran to them.

Oh, my gosh. You're wiped out. She looked Shay over, then Clarin. *Can you move?* No response. The telepathy had disappeared along with the kelling dimension. And so it would be, as with all expecting dragons, until the coming hatchlings got their own powers. It was one of the few limitations dragons had neither learned to overcome nor evolved from. When becoming parents—every time—they were simply a bit of a mess. At those times, the dragonkin relied upon one another. Now, the dragons relied on Diana and her humankin. Clarin used all her strength to sit up, trying to reassure Diana with the smallest nod of her head before she sank back into exhaustion.

Diana pulled out her phone, which registered a long list of missed calls and texts. The phone vibrated in her hand. It was her mother. "Mom, it's OK. We're OK," Diana gasped. She listened to the flash flood of "I was so worried; you didn't text back; how are the dragons; are you sure you're all right?" from her mother, followed by the insistence to know exactly where they were.

"We're by the creek on the other side of the hill from Illsworth's, close to that huge oak tree. The dragons just collapsed. They can't even move." She listened to her mom, comforted by her voice and her practicality. "OK, we'll stay by the oak and wait." Diana stood next to the dragons, her body providing their only shade. Dragging them under the tree was not an option.

Twenty minutes later, Linda Santos appeared on the horizon, carriers in hand. They loaded the tired heroes into the padded crates, Clarin and Shay each attempting to lend their last ounces of energy as well as they could. Linda offered them water, but the dragons could not even raise their heads. Diana and her mom headed the short distance to the road, their cargo borne awkwardly but surely by each of them.

"Are you all OK?" Linda Santos asked once they were loaded into the car.

"The dragons fell when the dark kelling stopped. But they knew it was coming, so they made me walk and they were flying really low. I don't think they're hurt." Diana was suddenly so tired herself, she could barely get the rest of the words to cross her lips, "They looked fine until then." She was too tired to tell the whole story. She looked back at the carriers harnessed in the hatchback. The dragons were completely still. Diana took a deep breath, heaviness seeming to replace the air. Before sinking into the car cushion and falling asleep, she told her mother, "We're all fine. But we're in a lot of trouble. Illsworth is up to something, something bad…" And she was asleep.

~

The remaining eggs were safe. Nicki left them in Diana's hat, pushing the brood into a far corner of the deep cement sill that ran the perimeter of Dr. Kim's dingy, but tidy, basement. A few inches from the warm, radiating brood, lay their cold, lost sibling, still wrapped in tissue. Nicki stood guard stoically, shielding them from any shred of light. Dr. Kim brought bags of grass and straw and filled the ledge to make the new nest. She tried to assure Nicki that the eggs were safe, that she should come upstairs and try to relax. Nicki would not be lured from her post. "I'll come up when Diana and the dragons get here, thanks," she told Dr. Kim, accepting a glass of orange juice.

Dr. Kim went back to her light-filled kitchen, closing the basement door behind her. She tucked her hair behind her ears in one fast motion. It was her only nervous habit, and pointless, since the hair always popped right back out. She looked out the window, searching for the Santos's green wagon. She saw only patchy asphalt and blotches of violet bursting from the ice plant lining the road.

Dr. Kim again descended the wooden basement stairs. "I'm back—needed to find something dark and heavy to cover this window." Nicki didn't bother to answer. Though neither had experience in helping to prepare for dragon hatchlings, all of those close to Diana knew the basics: no light. In fact, total darkness for many things dragon seemed a must. "I could use a hand," Dr. Kim said, while holding up the draping.

Nicki pushed the eggs further into the corner and adjusted the bandana and loose grass, then obliged, one eye still on the eggs. She held the black velvet fabric up while Dr. Kim drove fine nails into the window frame at close intervals, almost all the way around the square.

"Not taking any chances," Dr. Kim mumbled through the nails she held pursed in her lips.

"Right," agreed Nicki. "These babies deserve the best. It's sad enough about that little one," she said as her eyes floated to the tissue-wrapped bundle, "and they're not even going to have their big brothers and sisters around..."

"Chin up, kiddo. We may find those five sooner than you think. It's certainly a good start that their parents are back," Dr. Kim said.

"That's true," Nicki perked up. "I hope they're back in time for the hatching of the additions to their very large family."

"Won't they be surprised?" Dr. Kim smiled, then paused her hammering and continued to speak, this time sounding far away, "I do wonder what they went through to get back here...and where all the others are..." Dr. Kim resumed her tapping. "Poor Diana must be beside herself over her dad." She stopped her work. "There. Just a little flap in case we need to see out."

"Maybe she hasn't had much chance to think about it yet. Oh, I wish they were back already. There's just so much to—" Nicki's sentence was interrupted by loud knocking from upstairs.

"I'll go," said Dr. Kim. "I know you want to stay right where you've been." Nicki smiled gratefully. She returned to the hat of eggs and lightly placed her hands around it, feeling the reassuring heat.

Diana stood on the porch with her mom, the dragons still in their carriers. Dr. Kim opened the door wide. "Come in, come in. Oh, my..." She could see through the mesh that the dragons each lay in a heap. "Oh, my," Dr. Kim murmured again as she helped get the party inside. "Let's carry them right downstairs." She stooped to the carrier and whispered, "Your eggs are safe, dears. Nicki has not left their side." At this, Shay opened his eyes just enough to meet Dr. Kim's for a moment; and Clarin's sigh, for all its shallow fragility, seemed to fill everyone's lungs.

They carried the dragons downstairs, Nicki shining the elucifier over to light their way to the interior. Nicki and Mrs. Santos opened the carriers on either side of the eggs, and both parents drew themselves up with haggard reserves of strength to settle around the cluster of eggs, weary travelers finally home.

Diana stood close by and whispered, "I'll take them out and put them between you." She turned to Nicki and instructed her friend, "Keep the 'luce shining right on the hat," though Nicki automatically did so. With the care of a girl handling the fragile dragon eggs of her closest dragon friend, Diana removed each one, counting it and placing it in the grass. She reached eleven and smiled. Then, along with the rest of the humans and dragons, she gazed over at the cold, lifeless egg. "What about...? What about—?"

Clarin cocked her head to the side and gave a long, slow, peace-filled nod. "I'll leave it there," Diana sighed.

"We're so sorry," added Linda.

"Let's let them sleep," said Dr. Kim, her voice soothing.

At this, the dragons' exhaustion took over again and they dropped into a deep sleep. Diana was filled with longing and peace all at once, as the mistcrystal physically translated the now-synchronized heartbeats of the entire dragon family—parents and imminent children.

"Nicki! Thank you for getting the eggs here safely," Diana said when they were all back upstairs. They hugged each other, then Diana turned to Dr. Kim. "Thank you so much. I'm so glad you were home."

Dr. Kim looked sheepish. "Just when I vowed to start remembering to carry that phone...it was lucky I was home. I think I'll start relying less on luck and more on the technology at hand..." Dr. Kim trailed off, simultaneously pocketing the cell phone that lived almost exclusively at the end of its charger. Everyone gave a little laugh, though the mirth seemed to extinguish almost as soon as it materialized.

"Mind if I check the locks?" Diana asked, as they all moved toward the living room. She was already reaching for the front bolt.

"Of course not...I've already done it, but I know that won't stop you."

Diana ran to the side and back doors then met her mother coming down the hallway. "Don't worry, I just checked the windows in the bedrooms and bathrooms," Diana's mother said.

Diana headed to the kitchen and gave the bolt on the door directly across from the basement stairway a good rattling, though she had checked it when she came upstairs.

"All secure," she said to looks of no surprise. She sunk into the couch between her mother and Nicki and released a huge sigh. Her mother brushed at a strand of hair that had escaped Diana's thick ponytail. This time, Diana didn't object. She took a couple of deep breaths. "What now?" she asked of no one and everyone. All eyes were on Diana. She found the strength to tell them what happened at Illsworth's. She began wearily, but by the time she was explaining the strange devices on Illsworth and the vultures, she was reliving it as she told it. She ended her tale with the dying remark, "And not a clue about Dad."

Everyone was quiet. Nicki's soft voice slipped into the hush. "That reminds me: I found something kind of strange..." Diana sat up and leaned toward Nicki. Nicki reached into her pocket and pulled out the item, a wooden crescent about an inch and a half long. Now that she could see it, she knew it had something to do with the dragons. "Oh, my gosh," she said, and immediately handed the brown half moon to Diana.

Diana ran her fingers over the surface. It was incredibly smooth, with black streaks that blended almost imperceptibly into the dark chocolate color. It felt much heavier than a piece of pine or oak. She looked at it in disbelief. "Where did you get this?" she cried.

Nicki's heart raced. "In the nesting in the hideaway. I didn't have time to look at it in the cave, and I was so focused on the eggs I forgot about it until now. Why? What is it?"

Everyone was riveted on Diana as she turned and turned the mysterious object. "I don't know." Diana's voice went dry as she absorbed the magnitude of the coincidence, "But—" she pointed to a pearly beige inlay on what appeared to be the top of the curved artifact, "this symbol is in the missive." To this she got nods of recognition from everyone. "And it's the same as the one on Illsworth's nasty little devices." She handed the piece to her mom, who examined it and handed it to Dr. Kim.

"The wood reminds me of the little bird statue my dad brought back for me from a rainforest when I was little," Diana said.

Diana's father, an environmental anthropologist, went on many long trips to distant places, and brought enchanting little treasures back to his family. Diana's always involved some kind of animal.

"It's rainforest wood, all right, although they farm it these days. It looks like bloodwood from the flor amarillo tree. I've encountered it before: when working with your father in Venezuela," Dr. Kim explained. Everyone sat up taller; even the skimpiest connection between Jeff Santos and the current situation fanned their hope.

Diana and her mother shared a soft look for a moment before Diana refreshed her focus on the object: "And the symbol: it's in the missive."

"Right, the ouroboros: a dragon swallowing its own tail," said Dr. Kim, "a symbol of rebirth; it also stands for immortality. We saw it often in the villages we visited."

"And now it stands for *danger*, that's for sure," Diana said. They all began to speculate, carrying their conversation into Dr. Kim's bright kitchen where she was pulling out leftovers she insisted they try to eat. With these new connections to chew on, Diana's exhaustion disappeared. She ate and talked with gusto with the others, but in a hurry. They had a lot to do. They had a lot to figure out. And they had days, maybe a week , until the dragonlings arrived.

Diana slipped the wooden piece into one of her many khaki pockets and zipped it tight. She would examine it more closely soon. She left the room quietly. No one bothered her. In the basement, she sat on an old barstool with split padding, her arms on the ledge near the eggs, her head on her arms. Entranced by the heat of the dragons and the rhythm of her mistcrystal, she slept.

Chapter Six

A Restful Nest and the Rest of the Friends

They let Diana and the dragons sleep. Diana awoke in the early twilight, her body achy from her vigil by the nest, but the sleepy synchronicity of the mistcrystal and the dragon family's hearts reassuring her every fiber. She moved to Dr. Kim's couch. Diana slept past dinnertime and into the night, awakening twice with a start and running to look in on the dragons. Both times, they slept peacefully. It was helpful that dragons glowed faintly with each breath, so even though the mistcrystal told her they were safe, her eyes gathered visual reassurance. She crashed back to sleep and slept until the early light.

~

It was Sunday morning. Diana awoke suddenly. As in the night, it was too quiet. At her house, she had learned to sleep through her little brother's early morning cartoons and crashing toys. This quiet was startling. She sat up, now with some understanding of her mom's story of awakening in fright the first time Diana and Brody had slept through the night.

Diana crept to the basement door and opened it a crack. She heard nothing from downstairs. From down the hall she heard footsteps and doors opening and closing. Dr. Kim was up. Diana had just placed her hand on the knob to the basement door when she heard a knock. It was a soft knock, but she jumped like she'd heard a hammering.

Through the sheer curtain on the kitchen door she could see a dark brown face and kinky black hair. Huge brown eyes floated to and fro, filmy then solid, trying to see through the lace pattern of the curtains. The face belonged to twelve-year-old Jake Gonzales. Right behind Jake rose the form of his father in his khaki sheriff's uniform. The silver glint of his badge was visible beyond Jake's shoulder, where his dad's hand rested.

"Jake!" Diana said to herself in an animated whisper. She opened the door, beaming at her classmate and his dad. They were the only other people who knew about the dragons.

"Hey, Diana," he matched her quiet tone. Diana pushed at Jake's shoulder warmly.

"It's great to see you both," she directed herself toward Sheriff Gonzales now, too.

"How are you, Diana?" the sheriff asked. Diana shrugged and smiled. He didn't wait for more of an answer. "I got a call from your mom last night asking us to stop by. I understand we have some visitors?" Even the sensible, middle-aged lawman could not keep the excitement from his voice.

"Yes, it's Clarin and Shay and a new bunch of eggs," Diana enthused, though she kept her voice down. She looked at Jake. "I was going to text you right after I checked on them."

"I can't believe the dragons are really here," Jake said, awestruck. This past season, he had even given up baseball to spend more time helping decipher the missive; to spend more time immersed in the magic. His dad hadn't fought him on it, saying, "I never thought I'd see the day. But then I never thought I'd see a lot of things." Besides, Jake passed on the information he got to his dad, who was more than interested in any clues—though none really came—as to how and why Jeff Santos had not returned from his last expedition.

"Where are they?" Jake asked, awe in his voice.

"They're in the basement. You won't believe what they've already been through since they got back just yesterday." Jake and the sheriff hung on her every word as Diana retold the highlights of the experience with Illsworth.

"Whoa," Jake commented as Diana wrapped up her story.

"How are they now?" the sheriff asked.

"I was just about to check again." Diana could barely stand still. It seemed like days since she last saw them. "Do you want to come down? They'll be glad to see more allies." Jake nodded.

The sheriff started to nod as well, then switched tacks and said, "Don't let me hold you up. I'll just start the coffee for Dr. Kim. I think I remember where she keeps it." Sheriff Gonzales winked. Everyone knew he was a coffee fiend.

Sheriff Gonzales took a ceramic crock out of the cupboard, apparently determined not to horn in on the kids' experience, though eager to encounter the unbelievable creatures.

"Where I keep what?" Dr. Kim walked into the kitchen and hugged the sheriff. "Long time no see, Max. I see you still remember where I keep the good stuff. Hi there, Jake." She directed herself to Diana, "So how are they?"

"They seemed fine overnight. I hope they're not awake yet." Diana paused and looked around for Nicki.

"Her mom picked her up while you were sleeping," Dr. Kim said. "She said she'd be back this morning. Your mom will be, too."

She sent a quick text to Nicki, anyway, asking her to come over as soon as she could, then led the way quietly down the steps.

Clarin was just raising her head when Diana and Jake dismounted the creaky staircase, the elucifier in Diana's hand, giving them just enough light. As always when Diana was in range, their eyes met instantly. Diana walked to Clarin and stroked her. "Good morning. Are you alright?" It was second nature to speak to the dragon, whether there were barriers to telepathic responses or not. Clarin nodded and her eyes formed a slight smile, then travelled to Jake.

"Hi, Clarin," Jake said, his voice quiet and a little shaky, his eyes wide. His tone and posture might have suggested fear or trepidation, but a terra dragon never depended on the traditional senses to recognize a friend. Terras read the heart. Clarin tilted her head and leaned toward Jake.

"She wants you to go to her," Diana said, prodding Jake lightly in the back. Jake stepped toward the dragon. Clarin stretched her snout out, and Jake reached forward tentatively while looking to Diana. "It's OK. Go ahead," Diana said.

Jake stroked Clarin's snout and smiled. "Wow, so awesome. You're really real."

"Of course they're real. I knew you thought I made it all up," Diana teased.

"Come on, no way," Jake shot back. "But even with the magic wall...seeing them in person...it's unreal." They laughed at that, Clarin watching them with satisfaction.

Diana's phone buzzed. "Nicki is on the way with your breakfast: red worms and a special surprise," Diana said to Clarin, reading the text as she spoke.

Jake tapped Diana. Shay was stirring. He raised his head and nuzzled Clarin, then greeted Diana by stretching his neck out a bit, an invitation for her touch. Jake stepped closer. Shay's eyes were bright. "Hey, it's nice to meet you, Shay," Jake whispered happily. "I've read a lot about you." Shay seemed to smile. "And you're gonna be a dad soon," Jake said. He immediately blushed and stammered, "Uh, I mean...again..."

Diana touched his arm and whispered, "Don't worry about it."

He gathered himself and bent toward the eggs with Diana. She looked at Clarin, who turned her gaze toward the cracked egg, her smile gone. "The little ghost," Diana said. Grim silence filled the air.

"I'm really sorry," Jake said. He stood close to the lifeless egg.

Clarin and Shay looked from the child who would never be, to the nest of eleven who matured in their radiant armor.

"The *death kelling*—will you perform it now?" Diana asked.

Clarin and Shay shook their heads *no* in unison. Diana stood next to Jake. Before reaching for the little ghost shell, she looked at Clarin, who nodded. Diana picked up the egg and cradled it oh-so-gingerly. With her front claw, Clarin indicated a spot closer to the living brood. Diana placed the egg closer to the rest of its family, receiving a somber nod from each parent.

Diana turned back to Jake. "Well, it only makes sense to be extra grateful about the rest of these little ones," Diana stated, though not very convincingly, then added bitterly, "Illsworth could have killed them all." Diana walked back over. She carefully brushed away some of the grass.

"Wow. It's so intense," Jake said.

The eggs appeared to breathe electric breaths, brightening and dimming, each individual glow in sync with the breathing of the parents.

"Your mistcrystal is in sync with them all," Jake observed. Diana and Jake stared at the mass of eggs for a long time. It almost banished the sadness over the lost egg. Almost.

Their trance was broken by another text from Nicki. She was upstairs with the food. "Your breakfast is here," she told the dragons. It was hard for Diana to break away from her wonderment at the eggs, but she was excited to give the dragons their surprise. "We'll be right back."

Diana and Jake went up the stairs and found Nicki laying out mangoes and pineapple on a tray and pulling out odd-looking things from a bag. It was the homegrown surprise: tupi fruit.

Diana had planted the strange seeds her father had once brought back from the Venezuelan rainforest. At the time, her father had said that the locals had stories of magical creatures indulging in the fruits, their powers becoming exaggerated and uncontrolled under the effects of the delicious yield. Of course, these stories just represented fanciful legends—until the day Diana met Clarin.

Diana had planted those seeds two years ago. She had had to restrain herself from over-tending them. Starting the very day after planting, she would look for sprouts five or six times a day. Her mom had reminded her once that the seeds would take days to break ground, but Diana dashed from the house repeatedly anyway, checking and checking. Her mother let her be.

When the seedlings erupted, Nicki was over nearly every day, the two of them nurturing the thirsty rainforest plants. The fruit had finally come on last year and ripened, so she and Nicki had dried all they harvested. Now they had just picked some fresh from this year's crop. Diana couldn't wait for them to give this little welcome gift to the dragons.

There was no denying it: the fruit looked kind of creepy—like eyeballs: white, juicy, shiny orbs pierced by a black iris of a seed, all surrounded by the split russet-colored skin. Nicki piled up the tupi fruit, half fresh and half dried. The fresh stuff looked slimy; the dried stuff looked shriveled, like something the wicked witch from *Hansel and Gretel* might dehydrate and consume when she ran out of fresh children.

"What the heck?" Jake exclaimed, as he feigned retching. Diana and Nicki laughed while Nicki continued to pile the freaky fruits onto the tray.

"Hey, we worked hard to grow the tupi fruit for the dragons!" Diana chided.

Jake looked chagrined. "I know, I should've helped with the gardening." The girls rolled their eyes as if to say, *Like you would've*, while he rolled his eyes and said aloud, "As if."

Nicki continued, "I researched the tupi fruit. It's a main ingredient in those energy drinks our parents won't let us have."

Diana added, "We're pretty sure the dragons are crazy for it; you know, like your dad is for coffee." Understanding broke over Jake's face and the three laughed together. Jake's dad peeked over the kids' shoulders, coffee in hand.

"That is odd," he smiled.

"Come down and meet them and see how they like it," Diana said.

They headed toward the stairs. Jake was in charge of the red worms, which he was poking at with his fingers.

"Do you have to do that?" Diana asked, a shiver running through her.

"Sorry," Jake said, insincerely, as he kept poking at the seething pile.

"Hey, you two," Nicki greeted the dragons, "look what we've got for you." Clarin and Shay had already caught sight of the tupi fruit. The dragons' eyes popped open. Diana and Nicki exchanged a satisfied glance. The sheriff hung back and waved stiffly, incredulous at the magnificent creatures, and mumbled, "Well, I believed it, but I didn't *believe* I believed it. Now I do." He sipped his coffee and watched intently as the youths interacted with creatures his mind tried to keep believing he was seeing.

Their appetites piqued, the dragons still demonstrated their innate restraint by eating the worms first—Diana looked away, disgusted—followed by the fresh pineapple. When they got to the tupi fruit, Shay inserted his beak into the pile and counted them out, giving Clarin the extra one. Once they set upon the unexpected delicacy, their restraint disappeared quickly, as did all of the bizarre-looking fruit.

As Diana watched her friends indulge, she looked over at Nicki and mouthed, "High five." Nicki beamed.

"I've gotta try me some of that," Jake said.

"I don't think so," Diana retorted, then laughed.

Breakfast over, Clarin and Shay looked gratefully at their young stewards, their eyes brighter, their carriages straighter. Diana's heart swelled. The dragons began to settle into the straw.

"They need more rest," Diana said. She turned to Jake and Nicki. "Let's go, you guys."

"See you later—bye," Jake and Nicki chimed as they and the sheriff followed Diana back up to the light.

In the dark, quiet basement, the dragon parents hovered over their eggs. Occasionally, they would gently push their beaks into the straw to touch the fiery shells, sending a pulse of energy through them that momentarily brightened Shay's azure and his mate's amber scales.

Once in the kitchen, the three youths started talking immediately. "They loved the tupi fruit!" Diana effused.

"Yeah, they did! It's good to see them looking better," Nicki added, "but the *ghost*. It's too sad..."

Jake broke in, "Yeah. Illsworth needs to pay."

Diana reached into her pocket and held up the wooden crescent. It was the shape and depth of a tangerine slice, but even, flat, and smooth. Nicki and Jake dropped their original thoughts and concentrated on the object. "What the heck *is* this?" Diana mumbled.

"Uh, yeah, what the heck *is* that?" Jake mimicked, gawking, before it registered that it was the strange item from the end of Diana's story. The adults' voices drifted in from the living room. Diana slid her fingers over the polished wood. As she did so, she felt a slight irregularity. She held the wood up to her eyes. Within the wave of the tan and brown grain, she detected a curving, continuous line: a seam.

"I think it opens!" Diana cried, excited and frustrated at the same time as she tried to slide the box open. It wouldn't budge. The seam went all the way around the edge, yet it did not give, no matter which way she applied pressure. She handed it to Nicki, who tried in vain, then handed it to Jake.

"Let's show my dad," Jake suggested after his efforts also failed. They went into the living room. Dr. Kim and Sheriff Gonzales looked up from their conversation expectantly. After the young people reported on the state of the dragons, they handed over the box. Sheriff Gonzales commented on the inlay, which looked like mother of pearl, but darker.

"Oh, wow! It looks just like Clarin's—well, a terra's— scales," Diana exclaimed, mocking a slap of her forehead as she wondered how this hadn't been obvious to her before.

As Jake and his father listened to Dr. Kim and Diana explain the design, they showed no surprise at the heavy symbolism it held.

"I'm sure it opens," Diana said, as she took back the crescent. Neither the sheriff nor the retired scientist made any headway with it. "When they're more rested, I'll show it to the dragons. They must know something."

"A mystery to lead to more mysteries," Sheriff Gonzales said, the voice of someone accustomed to digging for answers. He handed the box back to Diana. Just then his radio went off.

"We have a 415 in progress. 42 Huerta Street."

"Darn. I was just about to beg you to let me peek at those dragons of yours again," the sheriff winked, "but danger and duty call. Mr. Gioberti is vacuuming the neighbor's rocks again." Sheriff Gonzales smiled as he left, followed out the door by everyone else's chuckling.

Chapter Seven

The Firesaving

The dragons were fed and the eggs were ensconced. Normally, one of the parents would leave the nest for a time to forage and stretch his or her wings. But after the harrowing journey to Pasqual Valley, the dragons would rely on their generous human benefactors. Still, Clarin had something she must do.

Clarin mustered her strength and approached the ledge. Her telepathy gone, she tried to summon Diana via subtle impulses within the mistcrystal. She was confident of the strength of their connection.

Diana appeared at the head of the stairs, crescent in hand, filled with the questions she somehow *knew* Clarin would answer.

Clarin was already looking to her. Jake followed Diana into the darkness, and the two helped Clarin rise as gracefully as she could from the nest. Clarin pulled her wings in tightly to navigate the steps on her strong but weary legs.

The awkward party entered the kitchen, Clarin heading straight for the back door. Jake ran ahead to open it, rushing out to check that the way was clear.

"Is it too risky to go outdoors?" Dr. Kim asked. Linda Santos murmured her agreement. Diana shook her head and stayed close to Clarin, saying flatly, "We follow Clarin."

Nicki and the adults followed. "Well, I suppose we've got plenty of cover from the shrubbery," Dr. Kim added.

The party exited the back door. Clarin managed a brief open-winged float down the few steps. Diana looked around nervously; Jake and Nicki instinctively flanked the house to be sure there was no one around.

"It would be a bad time for the electric company to send the meter reader," Dr. Kim said, as she, too, looked all around.

Diana held the box to her ear. "The box is humming," she said. The heat in Diana's mistcrystal increased with the hum. Clarin walked through the yard. Diana followed. As she got closer to Clarin, the heat and sound grew. "I knew you'd be the answer," Diana cried.

Diana threw her arms around Clarin, causing her tired friend to wobble on her feet.

"Oh, sorry!" Diana backed up, kicking herself mentally—it was just so hard to think of Clarin as frail.

A noisy truck passed on the road in front of the house, and the group's anxiety waxed and waned with the approaching and retreating grind of the engine.

Clarin led the way to the side of Dr. Kim's large shed. She stood with her back to the aging wood and settled with her wings open toward Diana. Diana's mistcrystal thrummed with extra life. She held the buzzing crescent tightly; even with her trust in Clarin, her heart began to mirror the disquiet of the object.

"Something is certainly up," Dr. Kim remarked, taking a place a few feet from Clarin's side.

"I'm sure it's fine," Mrs. Santos said, sounding not at all sure.

Diana moved completely into Clarin's reach, and Clarin encircled her in her wings, though she did not touch her.

"Hey, this is something from the wall," Jake whispered to Nicki.

"From the *missive*," Nicki replied authoritatively.

"Yeah, yeah..." Jake said.

"It's the firesaving..." Nicki said, eyes wide, her voice quiet but ringing of grandeur.

Clarin's eyes burned bright. As the fire caused her eyes to glow more and more gold, the four observers stepped back and formed a half circle. Jake had been talking about keeping watch around the side of the shed, but he joined the semi-circle, drawn in by Clarin's gaze, which moved from one person to the next, until it was lost somewhere distant.

Diana sat cross-legged like a small child, facing Clarin, the crescent cradled in her hands. She looked into Clarin's eyes, which met hers. Diana's heart calmed. She felt the warmth from Clarin's scales. They began to take on a deep glow, as if each scale was its own muted ember. The golden accents on Clarin's crest brightened. She began to look as if she could turn into fire herself, yet by a slow, deliberate ignition. Diana felt safe, protected. A calm anticipation welled up inside her.

The mistcrystal was more alive than it had ever been. It actually seemed to hum in unison with the crescent. Though Diana was vaguely aware of the others, everything outside Clarin's reach became a separate world. The temperature within the firesaving circle rose, yet the wooden crescent stayed cool—the wood now felt heavy and hard in Diana's hands. She ran her fingers over the inlay—the pearly material was quite warm.

The build-up behind Clarin's scales gave way to a slow, seeping heat from every part of her. Luxurious warmth permeated Diana *from the inside out*. She felt it everywhere; it seemed to go right through her, yet she knew she would not be burned. She wondered if she was glowing. *I feel like Clarin looks*, she thought.

The box lay across Diana's open palms. Now the chill of it felt stark and strange. The contrast between the cold box and her hands, as she shared the dragon's fire, made her want to drop it. Just then, she felt the coolness draining from the wood, replaced by a growing warmth that emanated *from inside the box*.

Diana sat perfectly still, her concentration centered on the strange sensations seeping into her. Her hands trembled. Or that's what she thought at first. It was not her hands. It was the box. She felt it distinctly: the dark wood quivered in her palm, on its own. The shuddering picked up. Now the box shook— practically jumped—in her hands. She felt a fleeting panic, an instinct to hold the box tightly, to quell its crazy quaking. But Clarin's presence overrode the uncertainty. Diana loosened her grip on the box, allowing the firesaving to continue to overtake her. The crescent danced on her hands.

Diana felt like fire itself—if fire had only light and heat but didn't consume. Clarin stood motionless. Each of her scales looked like an individual sun. Her irises expanded, obscuring her black pupils so she looked out from golden, blazing orbs.

Diana heard a faint crack—no, more like a tear. The box was splitting. That didn't seem right, it was so beautiful. Clarin's firesaving healed; it did not destroy. *What was going on?* The cracking sounds continued. The wood began to splinter on two sides. Mist and tepid dampness escaped from inside and kissed Diana's palms.

And then, something reached out from the box. One slender tendril extended itself to encircle the broken vessel, a tiny ark aground in Diana's hands. Seedlings, delicate and green, rapidly emerged from the disintegrating wood and wound around Diana's hands. Before her eyes, each curling stem sprouted tiny, feathery leaves.

As the plant continued to push its way into the light, it grew at lightning speed, fed by the firesaving magic. Within minutes, Diana had a lap full of greenery with comical, elephant-ear shaped seeds dangling from the thickening stalks. The plant was as warm as the fiery air. She brushed the continually erupting foliage gently, hardly able to distinguish the feel of it from her own skin. She looked at Clarin, whose eyes held their still focus on some unknowable point. The plant continued its uncanny growth; the soft leaves tickled Diana's arms and legs, while the branches draped over her and crept out of the firesaving circle.

Diana tingled with life and expansiveness, as if she were part of the plant herself. Then, in an instant, as if Clarin bore an "off" switch, her scales dimmed and turned back to their normal luster. The heat dissipated to the dragon's normal warmth. Her crest and eyes regained their usual golden tints, and the black pupils reasserted themselves within her amber irises.

The spring air rushed in and surrounded Diana. She shivered as though she'd been whipped with a wintery wind and instinctively gathered the plant to herself to protect it.

The main stalk was about an inch in diameter. Diana cradled it, along with the bits of broken box lying in her lap. The bisected dragon inlay was looking up at her. She was suddenly aware of everyone else looking at her, too. They all moved in closer.

"You were glowing, Diana! That was bomb," Jake cried.

Linda and Dr. Kim simply stared, examining Diana and Clarin for any signs of distress. Clarin slumped, but eyes alert, she followed all. She gave the adults a nod: she and Diana were fine.

"Oh, my gosh. I've never seen such accelerated metabolic activity," Nicki said, her eyebrow arching.

Jake shot Nicki a puzzled look. "Uh, OK, yeah, that was serious. You looked like you were on fire, Diana. And the tree: total fast-forward!"

Dr. Kim and Mrs. Santos zeroed in on the plant. "It's beautiful," Linda said, reaching out to stroke the downy leaves. "I wonder what it is..."

"I believe," Dr. Kim looked closely at the plant, "that it's a Venezuelan caro caro, also called 'elephant ear' tree." Dr. Kim reached for the seeds so that the funny-shaped pods lay across her fingertips. "They grow in the same rainforests as the tree the box was made from."

"They do look like elephant ears!" Jake said. "Cool."

Finally, Diana spoke. She felt like she'd been in a dream and only now had fully awakened. "We have to plant it. Right now." She was connected to this new life. She tenderly held the roots up.

"Yes, those will want some soil." Dr. Kim said as she moved toward the shed door.

"Let's put it in a pot for now," Linda added.

"Yeah..." Diana assented, her speech slurred. She rose, still looking like part of the tree, verdant stems and leaves appearing to sprout from her tan, slender limbs. Her mother went to her side and supported her daughter, poking carefully through the greenery to grip Diana's elbow.

"Jake and Nicki, will you go around to the side of the shed and get the biggest pot you can find?" Dr. Kim already had potting soil in hand.

Jake and Nicki ran.

Diana felt the plant in her hair. It was still growing quickly, though not as fast as during the firesaving. Linda Santos pulled gently at the coiling plant, carefully freeing more of her daughter's face, then neck, and working her way down her arms to where Diana held the roots. The longest stem wrapped around Diana's back like a friend's embrace. With each meticulous redirecting of the tenuous greens, the healthy foliage bounced back around its own slim branches.

They all helped in submerging the roots in the soil. Diana ran to get the hose and was about to sprinkle the soil with water when Jake shot his hand out and exclaimed, "What the heck?"

"What?" Diana said, trying to raise the hose in spite of Jake's block. This was a rainforest plant, possibly from a place her father had been—maybe where he still was. She had felt her father's presence during the firesaving. "It needs water right now!" Diana cried.

"But look," Jake said, one gentle hand on Diana's arm, the other pointing to the expanding stalk. Bark was forming before their eyes, turning the stalk from green to brown, except there was a strange—very strange—unevenness to the pattern of the bark.

"Whoa," said Nicki, as she stared.

"You can say that again." Wonder replaced uncertainty in Diana's voice.

"Whoa. That looks like...like...no way..." Everyone was leaning in, squinting. Diana continued, incredulous, "It is. It's writing..."

Chapter Eight

Reveal Interrupted

Diana's words of discovery hung in the air. The others leaned in closer, dumbfounded, as script continued to appear in the bark.

"Is this for real?" Jake asked. No one replied, rapt as they were at the impossible emergence of letters in the thickening trunk of *a tree.*

Diana looked over at Clarin, who took a step toward Diana from where she had remained so still since the firesaving. Haltingly, the dragon attempted another step, but she faltered, her front feet buckling.

"You guys!" Diana shouted, running to the depleted dragon. Jake, Nicki, and Mrs. Santos ran to Clarin's side.

"I can carry her," Jake insisted, and started to pick up their flailing friend like he did his yellow labrador.

"Careful of her wings," Nicki said, while Diana and Mrs. Santos reached out to help Jake position his hands safely around Clarin.

"Stay with the tree, OK?" Diana shouted to Dr. Kim, as she followed along while Jake turned to carry Clarin to the house.

"Of course. And Perhaps—"

Dr. Kim's reply was interrupted by a crack of lightning that split the air between her and the tree. The branches shook wildly; leaves flew into the air, some burnt and ripped by the intruding force. Jake ran to the house with the collapsed dragon, while Diana, Nicki, and Mrs. Santos ran toward Dr. Kim, their eyes to the sky and hands over their heads.

"No, Mom," Diana shouted, ducking and checking the sky. "Go with Jake and Clarin. Make sure she's OK!"

Linda Santos ran toward the house and jumped ahead to open the door as Jake approached the back stairs. The two disappeared into the house with Clarin.

The sound of wind—or wings—disturbed the air above Diana. She waved and grabbed at nothing, her fist briefly striking something warm and slick. Dr. Kim shouted for the girls to get behind her, but Diana stayed in front of the tree, her feet planted atop a patch of scorched ground where the attacker had first fired its—

Its what? Diana thought.

Nicki pointed above the tree and shouted, "Look!" Diana spun around to see a second bolt of electricity rain down, seemingly from thin air. Dr. Kim had picked up the plastic lid to a waste can, which she thrust above the tree, blocking the force of the current that melted a frisbee-sized hole in the green lid.

"It's after the tree! Grab something!" Diana ordered, looking into the shed and picking up a wooden-handled garden shovel.

"Nothing metal!" Dr. Kim shot back. Nicki armed herself with another plastic trash lid, though she knew it would be single-use only.

Jake appeared at the steps just in time to see the second bolt aimed for the magical tree. He looked frantically for an object that would shield or protect the tree and his friends. Nothing.

He ran to the shed and took a garden hoe, then to the tree, snapping up the last two trash can lids on his way. He heard the flapping in the air. "Here it comes again," he shouted, holding the hoe and lid like a sword and shield. He tossed Diana the other lid and then watched, horrified, as something invisible pulled up on her hair, lifting her to her toes, then letting go. Diana ducked and threw her hand to her head. Something sharp sliced into her. She cried out in pain as blood ran down her forearm.

"Diana!" Jake shouted, but stood his ground.

"I'm fine," she called back, though she trembled visibly as shudders of fear climbed up and down her spine. They stood around the tree, Diana mustering all the calm she could, their makeshift armor and weapons ready. Another sizzling current exploded above them, searing two of the shields.

"We can't keep this up," Nicki shouted.

"I've got it!" Diana yelled back. Diana realized what—who—it was. Recollections from the missive ran through her mind. "Dr. Kim," she shouted, "do you have a large flashlight or floodlight or something?"

Another blow landed on Diana, this time a scratch to her upheld arm. She dropped her shield and fell to the ground, grabbing her arm in response to the searing pain. "Stay down," Jake commanded. "I'll cover you."

Dr. Kim ran for it, calling back, "I have a power light in the garage, but you'll never find it fast enough."

Linda Santos ran out of the house and was beckoned by Dr. Kim to follow her to grab and plug in the orange extension cord. "Right there," she pointed at the outdoor outlet on the back of the house.

"We can only take one more blast," Jake said. "We need some other shielding."

"Don't worry," Diana said, getting back to her feet, she and Nicki combing the immediate sky for any signs. "The light, it will—"

The next blast came from a lower position, to the side. Nicki heard the crackling air and threw Diana behind her just in time. The flux of electricity liquefied most of the lid in her hand and she dropped it before the hot plastic could get to her skin.

Diana swung the shovel in the direction of the blast. It met something mid-air, but barely.

"Everyone get in here," Jake shouted, his sad plastic shield the only shelter left. Diana stooped to the plant, helpless but needing to defend it. Nicki slipped to Diana's side shouting,"Let's tip it so it's less vulnerable," and the two girls tipped the massive terra cotta pot on its side, Nicki reaching forward to press the roots in where the loose soil spilled out the top. Jake straddled the horizontal plant, and the two girls huddled under his slim but gallant protection. Diana placed the shovel scoop over Nicki's head and her own.

Dr. Kim and Mrs. Santos were in the yard. Linda ran to plug in the long cord when she was pushed forward from the back. Pin-pricks of blood, then streaks, began to appear on her shoulder through her thin, light blue shirt. She stumbled across the last bit of ground and knelt to plug in the cord. Dr. Kim flipped on the floodlight beam and began sweeping across the area around the tree. It shone faintly in the settling twilight.

Another charge of lightning shot toward the girls and the outstretched tree. Jake lunged above them with the shield, which was immediately melted in half. Dr. Kim swung the light toward the origin of the blast. In the path of the floodlight, a flicker of a body appeared for just a moment.

"Keep the light on it!" Diana shouted, as Dr. Kim circled the light beam around the last visible position of the assailant. Again, they saw a form, this time long enough for Dr. Kim to follow. She stepped in front of the kids, while Linda Santos ran to their sides. The light was on it again. It was as they had all feared— *known* really.

"AYAN!" Diana heard herself cry out, her horror at the confirmation combining with sickening denial. "No," she said quietly, tears brimming.

It was their ghost dragon, Ayan, Clarin and Shay's first-born, missing since his disappearance two years ago, along with his four siblings and Diana's father.

He turned in the air, followed by the light, which now disrupted his invisibility completely. Wobbling a bit, he careened toward the tree again and breathed a much less scorching stream of electricity toward the trunk.

Diana easily deflected the burst with the front of the shovel, sending it sputtering out in the direction of the shed. "Watch him—he's not finished," Diana warned as she wielded the garden tool, Jake at her side. Dr. Kim advanced with the disabling light.

Ayan hovered momentarily, wings beating unevenly. "Ayan... Why?" Diana shouted through her tears, though her heart knew.

"What has Illsworth done to him?" Nicki's inquiry was nearly inaudible.

Ayan's brilliant translucence had been replaced by a grayish transparency. A dull pallor marred his normally radiant scales. And there, around his neck, lay the same device they had observed on Illsworth's vultures.

Their errant dragon comrade waffled back and forth in the air, looking pathetically for a new attack path to complete his mission. He circled around once, the light draining his powers, and flew pitiably toward them.

Diana stood tall, her body only yards from the dragon, and held up the mistcrystal—it glowed meagerly since Clarin's collapse—hoping she could somehow attract the dragon by her kinship. "Ayan! Please," she cried, as if she could reason with the tortured dragon son.

"Diana, no! He may have some fire left in him," Linda called, pulling her daughter back toward her. Ayan stayed his course, then pulled up, unable to regain his target. His flight faltered even more, and he dipped toward the ground before recovering enough to manage a clumsy hover. His eyes opened wide, his mouth gaped. The device around his neck emitted a series of high-pitched pulses. Ayan flapped his way out of the beam, nearly hitting the ground just yards from Diana.

"Ayan!" Diana started toward him, but quick restraint by her mother and friends anchored her to their sides.

"You don't know what Illsworth did to him, what he might do," Nicki reasoned, her voice both sad and steady.

"It's true," Dr. Kim added. "We don't know if he'll remain subdued." She put a hand on Diana's shoulder.

"Ayan..." Diana's insides sank, her voice cracked. The dragon beat his wings more steadily, hovered a moment as the women trained the light on him, waiting for his next move.

"Oh, I don't like to flood him with light again," Dr. Kim said.

The strange pulses from Illsworth's device sounded once again and Ayan flew off, shaky strokes propelling him over the nearby stand of trees.   Then   he   was   gone.

Chapter Nine

The Mystery in the Bark

They all stared at the last spot Ayan had occupied on the horizon, Diana on her knees, her eyes leaking tears. No one wanted to break the silence. Linda came to her daughter's side and guided her up from the grass. Diana let herself follow, her body leaden.

"We need to get that cut cleaned up," her mom said quietly. Diana, silent, began to back away, eyes on the sky, then turned and walked with her mother.

Dr. Kim, Jake, and Nicki gathered the remnants of their domestic weaponry. "Just toss the lids in the cans for now," Dr. Kim said, as she wound up the extension cord. Nicki stayed close to the plant, picking up a few items of debris around it. Diana shook herself a bit and broke from her mom, making a beeline for the plant.

"Here," Jake said, walking to the girls, "let's pick it up." His voice sounded much older. He and Nicki pulled the pot to its upright position. Diana immediately scooped up and deposited the soil atop the roots, patting it with far more concentration than the task really required.

"It looks good," Dr. Kim said. Diana bent down to look at the trunk while Nicki and Jake rotated the pot toward her view.

Mrs. Santos knelt by her daughter, her eyes searching the tree and her daughter's profile. "What's going on?"

"Mom, when I was in the firesaving circle, I felt Dad the whole time. It was like he was right there with me." Everyone looked at Diana, then stooped to see the tree bark.

"Then maybe Clarin was still with Jeff," Linda Santos exclaimed in a voice that seemed to reach desperately for the possibility; then, regaining her normal voice, she finished, "before they came back." Everyone looked at her, then the tree; no one spoke for several long moments.

Diana's hand shot to her neck. "Clarin's awake," she said, with at least a tinge of brightness. Then she sank down onto her knees, her hand on the subtly stirring mistcrystal. "If we just had our telepathy..." Dr. Kim placed a hand on her shoulder. Diana sat up, her eyes on the stalk. "It looks like "B-e—,'" she said, peering at the cursive line. She stood.

"We have to take the tree inside," she all but ordered. The rest chimed in their agreement.

"The greenhouse would be ideal. But I have a sunny spot in the living room," Dr. Kim said.

"We can do a search for what this kind of tree needs," added Nicki.

"Besides a rainforest. And magic," Jake added, then blushed lightly at his sarcasm at such a time. Diana looked to him and, to his relief, gave a slight smile.

"I'll get the plant," Jake said, wrapping his arms around the large pot.

"How about a hand?" Dr. Kim whispered to Nicki, who slipped in to support the bottom. Diana let herself smile. They all hovered around Jake to spot him as he lifted the treasured, but heavy, tree. He graciously gave in to the extra support up the steps and then carried the plant to the spot indicated by Dr. Kim. She and Nicki dashed back outside to bring in the light and cord. "Best keep this handy," Dr. Kim sighed.

"I'm gonna check on Clarin," Diana said, starting toward the basement.

"Not before that cut is cleaned," her mother said.

Almost on top of Linda's statement, Dr. Kim added, "Let's have a look at your scratches, too, Linda."

"It's nothing," Diana said and her mother said in unison.

"Sure. Come on," her mom said, raising an eyebrow.

Diana followed, knowing it was pointless to protest, and assured by the steady sensations from the mistcrystal that Clarin was at least mostly alright. "But it is weird. It *really* doesn't hurt," she said as she looked more closely at the five-inch gash on her outer forearm.

"That's really weird, too." Linda Santos pulled her daughter's arm over, looking closely.

"What? What's wrong?" Diana said, as her mother appeared to over-investigate. Diana's cut was fairly deep. It had stopped bleeding. In every way, it looked like a normal, deep scratch from a sharp object: red and a little raw, but straight. But the edges of her skin had a slight glow. "It looks like I got into that shimmering make-up powder I dumped all over the bathroom when I was five," she said.

Linda Santos held her daughter's arm close. She poked at the edge of the healthy skin around the wound. "Can you feel that?"

"Yes. It feels fine. I feel fine."

"It doesn't seem deep enough for stitches. Let's wash you up," her mom said, pulling her into the bathroom where Dr. Kim had already laid out the first-aid kit. The warm water and soap caused no protests from the patient, nor did the antibacterial cream. The shimmer remained on Diana's skin after the cleaning.

"It's kind of pretty," Diana said.

"It's kind of worrisome," her mother replied.

Diana knew that tone. She started out of the bathroom, then swooned a bit and had to steady herself on the wall.

Jake came running. "I bet turning to fire makes you super tired," he said, trying to make light of the situation but holding steady to support Diana.

"Yeah, it does. But not as much as fending off a poor, messed-up dragon who is really your friend," Diana answered. Her mother was behind them.

"You need to rest," she said.

"I need to see Clarin," Diana said, and headed for the basement.

The firesaving was very draining when a terra dragon was in full power; while expecting hatchlings, it was overwhelming. Clarin had been able to perform it now because Diana wore her mistcrystal, and they were encircled by the goodwill of trusted friends. Diana's own energy waned, and her injury would soon catch up to her, too. A small price to pay for evidence of her father.

Diana approached the nest to see Shay sharply regarding her. Diana stood between the dragons, turning to Shay. She said softly, "Don't feel bad. It all happened so fast. You couldn't leave the eggs with Clarin in this state. We're all fine, really."

Shay gestured with his snout toward Diana's arm; Clarin followed with her eyes. Diana held out her arm to display the strange wound. "Ayan," she said, remorseful at having to name their lost son, "but I'm totally OK." Shay leaned closer to nuzzle the glossy area of skin, as he exchanged a meaningful look with Clarin. Clarin, barely able to move, leaned her head toward Diana's arm. Diana offered it to Clarin. Clarin touched the skin with her snout, causing an immediate, momentary surge in the mistcrystal. *Was she imagining it, or did she feel a flash of Ayan somehow in that moment?* Her thoughts accompanied pangs of loss, but the dragon's expressions were inscrutable. Clarin dropped back down to her position of rest. Diana simply said, "Ayan," again, and with a last look at the dragons and their developing brood, she quietly left the basement.

In the kitchen, Dr. Kim and the others—minus Mrs. Santos—were eating. Fruits, veggies, bread, and cheese covered the table.

"Are they OK?" someone asked. Diana nodded.

"Where's my mom?" she asked, more interested than she could make herself sound, and walking toward the living room, her goal the overstuffed chair.

"She said to just rest. She had to pick Brody up from his play date," Dr. Kim said, following Diana into the living room with a plate of food.

"Too tired to eat. But thanks." Diana sank down and let the comfy chair cushions envelop her.

"Just a few bites." Dr. Kim set the plate on the end table.

Diana ate a piece of cheese. One bite and her stomach overrode her fatigue and she reached for more. She swallowed a few more bites, then snuggled into the fuzzy blanket Dr. Kim had just placed over her. Jake and Nicki came in. Her friends looked at the tree, squinting to try to make out the gnarled script in the twisty bark.

"Do you see that?" Jake said. "Another letter just appeared."

"Oh, wow. Oh, no. Oh..." was all Nicki could reply.

Dr. Kim looked. "I think we can all surmise what that will spell—"

They turned to Diana.

"Should we wake her?" Jake asked.

"No," Nicki and Dr. Kim said together.

"She'll need her rest." Dr. Kim shook her head.   "We   all   will."

Chapter Ten

Mystery Revealed, Mystery Created

Diana awoke with the dawning light touching her face, filtered by Dr. Kim's thin, lavender curtains. A moment's disorientation was banished by the strong pulse of the mistcrystal. Clarin must be feeling better, she thought, standing and tossing off the throw and another blanket that someone had laid over her.

As she stood, she became light-headed. Her stomach rumbled. She headed into the kitchen and found cereal, bowls, utensils, and fruit laid out with a note from Dr. Kim: "Eat anything you find. Wake me if I'm not up."

Diana grabbed milk from the refrigerator, poured it over some granola and wolfed it down, barely chewing. She poured a second bowl and ate at a normal pace. A few moments after the biting hunger had abated, her mind began to race. *The tree.* She dropped her spoon and dashed back to the living room, kneeling in front of the tree. Her jaw dropped. The first letters, "B-e," that she had seen yesterday, were now followed by the rest of the word, and another. Diana shuddered as she read "Beware

Ouroboros," but the true cause of the tingling along her spine came from taking in the next letters: a looping capital "I" followed by "l-l-s..." It may as well have spelled "chills."

Where was her phone? Where was everyone else? She found her phone, battery nearly drained, on the end table. It was barely 7:00 a.m. *They had to go home*, she thought, wanting them back. She texted Nicki and Jake. *Had they seen?* She texted her mom, from whom she received an immediate response. Diana let her mom know she was fine and not to rush over, thinking virtuously of her little brother not being abandoned again, but perhaps less virtuously of keeping her curious sibling at bay.

Her remaining breakfast abandoned, she ran to the basement stairs, slowing herself for the descent so as not to wake the dragons.

She flipped on the 'luce and made her way down. In the corona of light she saw Clarin's shining eyes. Her wings lay flat and drooping at her sides as she hunched over her front feet, her head low. But her eyes shone urgently. She pulled herself forward, as if to dismount the deep ledge. Diana ran to her. "Stay there! You are so worn out." She put her hand on Clarin's wing, the warmth of her scales transferring to the mistcrystal and Diana's heart.

Clarin inched forward, her eyes locked on Diana. "Hold on," Diana implored. She passed the 'luce over the eggs to ensure they were all covered, and adjusted a piece of straw needlessly. Then she dashed to the window, pulled back the drape, flipped off the 'luce, pocketed it, and ran back to her friend.

Shay was awake now, watching his mate. He rested his head near the eggs, his snout nearly inside the pile, eyes moving from Clarin to Diana. At a quizzical expression from Diana, he raised his head slightly, peace in his sapphire eyes, and nodded. Diana was worried about what yesterday's events did to Clarin, but Shay seemed to be assuring her she should follow Clarin's lead.

Diana helped Clarin down. The dragon all but collapsed on the floor. "What are we doing?" Clarin lifted a clawed foot onto Diana's knee, reaching almost like a child wanting to be picked up. A tear formed in Diana's eye. She picked up the dragon, holding her awkwardly at first, then shifting her easily onto her shoulder. "You're all scales and magic," she said, hugging the dragon to her.

Upstairs, Clarin looked extra small in the bright kitchen. Clarin indicated the direction of the living room. As they approached the tree, Diana's heart pounded. A voice behind her sent her jumping, clutching Clarin to her.

"Good morning." It was Dr. Kim, wearing a bathrobe over plaid pajamas, battered slippers on her feet. She rushed to help cradle the dragon, whom Diana was easing to the floor.

There was a quiet knock on the door. Dr. Kim peeked out, then opened it to admit Nicki and Jake, who had coordinated their arrival. "We stopped for these." Jake thrust a transparent container of red worms toward Diana, apparently unable to resist trying to get a reaction every time. Diana didn't mind, though. Diana quickly, gingerly set Clarin down and scooted away a bit, as she gestured to Jake to go straight to Clarin. Jake popped off the lid and held out the food. Daintily, Clarin consumed four or five bites of the squirming sustenance, then looked to Diana.

"Take Shay some breakfast, too?" she asked her friends. She handed the 'luce to Nicki, who left the room with Jake—and the worms—right behind her.

Clarin moved closer to the plant. She pushed herself up on her hind legs and spread her wings tentatively.

"What's going on?" Diana said.

Dr. Kim looked at the bark. "Last night," she regarded Diana, who was now supporting Clarin with a hand under her wing, "new letters appeared. You were asleep. And now, I see, another is forming."

Diana saw the tail after the *I-l-l-s*. "No doubt, that's gonna be a 'w'," she said, sounding disgusted.

"No doubt," Dr. Kim replied. She moved around to Clarin's other side. Clarin was raising her wings further and stretching them around the slender tree's trunk and branches. Dr. Kim pulled the pot away from the wall.

Clarin pushed her left wing out toward Diana, and Diana moved around to the other side of the tree. Clarin flicked her head toward Dr. Kim, managing a small, but warning, screech. Dr. Kim backed away.

"Looks like you're in for round two," she said. "Poor thing," she murmured to the teetering dragon.

The tree was about four feet tall now, with leaves and seeds, as well as fluffy white flowers reminiscent of dandelion seedheads. The new bark was beginning to darken.

Diana held both tips of Clarin's wings. When the circle was complete, the mistcrystal blazed. A burning aura took over the living room, though Dr. Kim remained cool. Clarin took a huge breath. She glowed as she had in the backyard firesaving.

Nicki and Jake entered at that moment, both slipping quickly to Dr. Kim's side, their faces fervid in the unnatural indoor radiance. Nicki muttered, "Oh, my gosh," and took out her phone to start taking photos. Jake looked at her questioningly. "She'll want the scientific—er, magical—documentation," she whispered, only half-defensively.

Clarin and Diana luminesced more intensely. The entire room burned danger-less-ly, as if lit by its own benevolent little sun. The tree shot up to seven feet or more, leaves and branches bending as they touched the ceiling. As the foliage spread over Diana, a branch full of feathery leaves, elephant-ear seed pods, and downy flowers draped over her shoulder and down her back. The bark on the tree thickened, appearing an even darker gray.

There was a mature caro-caro tree in the living room.

The glowing ceased suddenly. Clarin's scales went cold, and her body sank to the floor. Diana wavered on her feet, one hand losing its grasp on Clarin as the dragon collapsed. Dr. Kim, closest to Clarin, bent to the dragon, touched her side and breathed a sigh of relief. "She feels warm," she announced.

Diana echoed the sigh, and let her friends guide her to the soft chair. Her eyes, riveted on Clarin, dared to drift over to the tree.

Nicki turned to the dragon, "Oh, why did you do that to yourself again?" she questioned.

"For this," Diana said, sitting forward to stretch toward the tree trunk, and pointing. The air seemed thick. They all looked at the trunk. It was now about six inches around, and there was an entire line of script twisted in the bark.

Diana slinked from the chair to her knees. She ran her hands over the impossible letters, her heart pounding, mistcrystal racing, and eyes brimming. Her hand slipped as she lost her hold on consciousness. "Dad—" she uttered, then crumbled the rest of the way to the floor.

Dr. Kim dashed to Diana, feeling her pulse and forehead. She heaved a sigh and patted

Diana's cheeks. From somewhere, Diana found the strength to open her eyes. "Dad. Clarin..."

"It's OK, Diana," Dr. Kim said as she propped Diana's head on her knees.

"Is she OK?" Jake asked.

"She seems fine. She's in a little bit of shock, but it seems quite mild, considering." Dr. Kim sounded unsure, but after placing her fingers over Diana's pulse again, she nodded and smiled.

"Let's get Clarin to the nest," Nicki instructed. Jake didn't miss a beat in picking up the dragon. He and Nicki set Clarin down in the nest, Shay nuzzling her affectionately across the eggs. "I'm gonna stay down here with them for awhile," Nicki said.

"Good idea," Jake replied. "I'll go see what they need upstairs." The friends stood, silent for a moment, then Jake broke off and zipped up the stairs. He stumbled at the top.

"Oh, sorry!" Nicki called, shining the 'luce toward the stairs too late. Jake was already through the door.

Upstairs, Diana sat with her back propped against the couch. Dr. Kim had pulled the tree out in front of her, and sat on the couch, regarding it with Diana. Jake entered and sat

123

next to Diana on the floor, asking as he sat, "What does it say?"

He read it for himself, as Diana was replying, "Nothing good." Her voice sounded flat and distant.

"Oh, dear," Dr. Kim said.

"I knew it. That creep!" Jake exclaimed. Dr. Kim placed a hand on his shoulder. He quieted.

A soft knock on the door was followed by Linda Santos's admittance. She took in the fallen faces as she approached the tree with hesitant steps.

Linda peered at the writing in the bark. She gasped. She knelt by Diana and took her daughter's hand, still staring at the bark. "How can it be?" She sank to a seated position, leaning on Diana. "Jeff. It's...it's Jeff's..." She looked at her daughter's sunken face. "That's your dad's handwriting."

Chapter Eleven

Realizations

"Illsworth," Linda Santos said, her voice shaking, "What have you done?" By now they had all read the message to themselves. They were stunned, puzzled. Nicki read the words aloud, though they were fast becoming as ingrained in each of their brains as they were in the bark:

Beware Ouroboros Illsworth holds 5
Ayan Beware Azeru~~

The message trailed off in a scribbled line. Diana spoke. She sounded like someone else, weak and dejected. "Clarin and Shay's children. Do you think they've been right over there..." she gestured dejectedly toward Illsworth's, "...the whole time?" The room was still.

Then Jake exploded, "So what does it mean? Illsworth has all five of the dragons?" He stood with his hands clenched at his side, eyes narrowed, as he twisted his body in the direction of Illsworth's property and postured rigidly, like he was confronting the villain right from his spot on Dr. Kim's worn, braided rug.

Nicki rose from studying the tree, uncharacteristic gall in her voice. "And he's doing something terrible to Ayan!" She waved toward the tree, "And what's an 'Azeru—'?"

"Or who..." Dr. Kim said.

Linda Santos sat quietly, staring at her husband's writing in the tree bark. Dr. Kim placed her hand on her friend's shoulder.

The weariness left Diana as if flowing out through her feet. She stood up and spun around to face everyone, "So Ayan, Merac, Tethys—" her voice broke.

Nicki went on for her, "Tynan and Gryn..." before her voice faded away.

Diana gulped and spat out, "have been right over there *this whole time*?" She mimicked her earlier gesture, but now pointed her finger accusingly in the direction of Illsworth's property.

The energy sapped from her as quickly as it had appeared. Her hand dropped, her shoulders drooped. *All of Clarin and Shay's children, all five dragonlings, had been a mile away, for how long? Two years?* It was unthinkable.

Nicki faced her friend. "OK, he has them." She stood closer to Diana. "At least now we know," Nicki said, then looked at Jake imploringly.

"Right. We have something to go on. We can do something," Jake added, his whole body still on alert. He received nods from all but Diana, who had stood looking at her friends, blank but listening.

Dr. Kim stood and joined the little circle around Diana. She said gently, "Yes, the message clearly states that he 'holds five.' It almost certainly must refer to the dragons."

Diana's eyes brightened. She looked to each of them. Her mother stood, too, adding, "As for poor Ayan, we can see Illsworth's using him abominably," her voice was sad but determined. "But at least we know he's here and alive..."

The possibility that this might not be the case for the other four dragons—a sun, a sea, a ghost, and a terra—hit them all. Again the room filled with terrible silence.

Diana needed to be with Clarin and Shay. In the light of the 'luce, she went to them. Diana leaned in close to the nest and closed her eyes. She was met with quiet stillness from both dragons.

Then, something else. Something new. Clarin was scratching in the straw dust. A symbol appeared beneath her claw. Now too familiar, the sight gave Diana chills: *the ouroboros*, the dragon swallowing its tail.

Clarin drew a second symbol. "That symbol is in the missive," Diana said. "It means 'ancient magic.'" She pointed to two crescent moon shapes with a wing between them.

Diana looked back at the dust. Now Clarin etched a half-sphere, like a bowl, with four overlapping wing shapes seeming to lie within it. "That one's in there, too," she said, her finger hovering over the third symbol. "It means 'safe place.'"

Diana had had two years to memorize every dragon-glyph left behind by her father and Clarin. It had kept her going while she awaited their return. Nicki had transcribed all Diana had translated, and Linda Santos, Jake, Dr. Kim, and Sheriff Gonzales were all eager pupils of the secrets there.

Clarin drew a third pictograph: a simple circle with four dots at even intervals; then a fourth: a single wing with several vertical lines radiating from the top and a line underscoring it horizontally. Diana didn't understand the circle, but she shivered at the fourth as she said, "Sacrifice." Diana watched as Clarin drew a line connecting the symbols, so the four formed a square, outside of which fell the ouroboros. Clarin drew a small circle in the center, then reached forward and nipped at the mistcrystal. Diana put one hand on her mistcrystal, while she dotted the dusty circle with her other forefinger, looking gravely at Clarin.

Clarin nodded and looked to her mate. Shay had been watching the interaction intently. He remained motionless. A mist obscured the light in his sea-blue eyes as he regarded Diana, then Clarin.

Noise from above broke Diana's concentration. Someone was rattling the door. Diana heard it open and then abruptly close, followed by more rattling and a light, quick knocking, which immediately ceased amidst harsh, low voices.

What's going on up there? Worry ascending the steps with her, Diana reached the door and cracked it open. A hand jutted out and latched onto the side of the door. She heard her mother's exasperated voice, "Hold on— I said, hold on..."

Diana pulled the door knob hard toward her, while simultaneously wedging her toes in the gap to keep it from crushing the grabby fingers. She recognized the webbed red-and-blue superhero gloves immediately: her little brother, Brody. "What are you doing here?" Diana nearly hissed through the tiny gap of space she allowed between them. She imagined that the goodwill of Dr. Kim, 'who just adored that boy', would descend upon them any moment. But this was not a good time for super-spirited seven-year-olds. Brody pulled. He tried to wedge his head into the space, but only a messy shock of sandy reddish hair protruded into the opening.

"Brody. Take a breath," Diana heard her mother almost scold; then, directed at her, "Honey, you can understand why he's so excited. Could you come up and talk with him, please?" The way her mother dragged out the *pl-ea-ea-se* whittled at Diana's resistance.

"Please, let me in! I'll be good. I want to see the dragons!"

Diana let the door open enough to partially fill it with her indignant frame, directing herself at her mother, "*Mom*, why did you tell him already?"

Brody broke in, "Mom *didn't* tell me. I figured it out *all by myself*." He looked back at his mom. "I saw you putting the carriers in the car, and then Nicki asked me to help get a bunch of worms out of the composter." He grinned back at Diana and continued. "You've been gone *all* the time, and Mom let me play video games over at Luis's as long as I wanted, *and* she ordered pizza *two times...*" Brody finished his run-on explanation, triumphant.

Diana rolled her eyes and muttered, "Way to be obvious, Mom." Then, managing again to decrease the gap through which she spoke—though a piteously pleading fraction of Brody's face still jutted into it—she almost smiled. You didn't get much past him. "Look, Brody, I promise you can see them. Just come back later." Diana needed to finish whatever the dragons had started with the symbols in the dust. The boy's face fell. He sighed. She searched his little expression for any sign of resignation. None.

"Please. I promise, *cross my heart*, I'll be good." Something melted in Diana. She could see him when he was five years old, begging their dad to let him help hammer together garden boxes in the backyard. Poor Brody hadn't seen their dad in two years either. He could barely remember him. And of course he knew Clarin had appeared that day with their father, and he had missed it all. How could she keep him out?

Brody instantly read the softening of his sister's features. He began to bounce up and down on his toes. Diana opened the door just enough for her to slip through, closing it gently behind her and resting against it.

"OK, let's go!" Brody buzzed like a bee.

No way was Diana about to take him down there with this level of stimulation going. "OK, look. There are eleven eggs in the nest," Diana explained, her hand on Brody's shoulder. His eyes were wide. He was actually almost *still*. She continued, "We cannot let anything affect them. They are covered and need total darkness, and the dragons are exhausted and need us to be *calm*." With this last word, Diana attempted to bore her intentions into her brother by boring her gaze into his eyes.

Brody squeezed his hands together in front of him, as if he were trying to wring out his excitement. Diana's heart softened at his effort. Still, she would stay within arm's—no, hand's—reach.o of him to be sure. "OK, no sudden movements. No shouting. No trying to touch the eggs. You can't see them anyway."

Dr. Kim stepped into the kitchen and smiled brightly. "Brody, how nice to—"

The imploring look shot over by Diana was met with an immediate shift in tone. Dr. Kim continued, "Need another tour guide?" Linda, who had been watching her children's interactions with pride and satisfaction, gladly stepped away. Everything would be smoother without a mom in the room.

Diana, a hand on her brother's arm, opened the basement door. With her eyes, she begged Dr. Kim to go first. Brody followed, Diana behind him, lightly but firmly pinching the fabric of his t-shirt. As Brody hopped off the last step, a sigh escaped him. Dr. Kim, to whom Diana had already handed the 'luce, positioned herself beyond the dragons and their nest, lighting the way for the new visitor. Brody walked forward in deliberate steps, the awe of seeing real dragons apparently the remedy to his usual streak of movement.

Diana stepped to her brother's side, keeping a grip on his shirt sleeve, as he approached Shay first. He leaned in. "Wow," he breathed, "you are so cool." The boy leaned in closer. "I mean, warm." He giggled quietly at his own joke. He looked at Diana, while raising a tentative hand toward Shay.

"Don't look at *me*," Diana teased. Brody turned toward the azure dragon, who was reaching forward, inviting the boy's touch. Brody touched the black snout, then pulled his hand back slowly and stared at it. He ventured a stroke of Shay's wing. The dragon spread them out as much as possible next to the nest. "You look like a waterfall," Brody said, his precociousness showing. He stepped closer and Shay wrapped the edges of his wings halfway around the starry-eyed boy. With the arc of heat flanking him, his face awash in shimmery blue, Brody murmured, "And you feel like a campfire."

"Come to Clarin," Diana said, her mistcrystal warming with the triangle of connection among her brother, the matriarch dragon, and herself. All shyness vanishing, Brody popped himself in front of the shining, earth-colored Clarin, who nipped affectionately at his hair, right where it stuck up in the back.

"You look like the tiger's eye my dad gave me," he said to the dragon, running his fingers down the inside of one of her now half-crimped wings. He reached in his pocket and produced a polished stone, richly striped in the same palette as the dragon. Clarin gestured to the space next to her and tapped her snout to the ledge.

"She wants your tiger's eye," explained Diana.

"It's from Dad," Brody protested, though curiosity and a tingling feeling that his dad would encourage him caused him to surrender the stone. Clarin scraped at her claw, just above the black talons, causing a few golden scales to fall atop Brody's precious stone. She breathed a miniscule, concentrated beam of fire on the scales, liquefying them into a tiny puddle of gold.

"Cool!" Brody gasped, reaching for the altered tiger's eye.

Clarin's snout blocked him, as Diana exclaimed, "No, it's hot!" The dragon scooted the gem toward Diana, who leaned in and blew on it like their mother used to blow on Brody's oatmeal, then dabbed at it as Clarin looked on peacefully. Finally, she gave way to her brother's grabbing hand. He held it up and Dr. Kim shined the elucifier directly on it. The solidified scales adhered to one side of the stone, mimicking Clarin's scales exactly, and felt as smooth as the rest of the rock.

"Wow, thanks, Clarin!" Brody beamed nearly as brightly as his new winged friends glowed. He put the stone into his pocket. "I wonder what it does..."

"Something good, I'm sure," Dr. Kim said.

"Something magical," Diana said, her hand on her mistcrystal.

"Something awesome!" Brody exclaimed, throwing his arms around the wiry dragon and causing her a momentary imbalance. Diana leaned in to mediate the overzealous embrace, a remonstration about to leave her lips, when she heard movement behind her, near the stairs. In her peripheral vision, she saw a gray shadow zip behind a cardboard box. On the cement ledge—a deep shelf that ran all the way around the basement—a tin watering can lay on its side, still waffling to a stop in the wake of whatever had overturned it.

"What it is?" Diana half whispered, half shouted to Dr. Kim, who was already pushing past the two children in search of the source of the disturbance. Diana swept the suspicious area with the beam of her 'luce, her heart racing. The indistinguishable intruder rounded the corner and was now halfway to the dragons. Diana rushed to the ledge in an attempt to block the path to the nest. She shined the light in front of her as she heard Dr. Kim's exasperated voice: "Oh, Dashwood!"

It was Dr. Kim's cat. Diana sighed with relief but stayed in position, eyes peeled. She couldn't risk the cat getting near the eggs. "He must have slipped in when we all came down." Dr. Kim summoned the errant feline with the kissing sound that meant a tuna treat was coming, and the cat instantly ran to her. As Dr. Kim bent to pick up the gray tabby, Diana laughed quietly, though uneasiness still churned in her stomach. She wiped some sweat from her brow and started to turn to her brother, who was frozen to the spot, leaning toward Clarin for security.

"It's OK," Diana assured him, midway around, taking her time to run the elucifier over the quiet nest, her stomach pangs nearly quelled. At that moment, a shattering squeal cut through the dark, basement air. Diana spun the rest of the way to face her brother, shouting, "Brody! What did you do?!"

"It's not me!" he cried, the bewilderment and fright on his face making him look like a baby again. "What is it, what is it?!" he shuddered.

Diana shot the few feet to his side. The reality of what she was hearing permeated her, as did the sudden energizing of her mistcrystal. It all but ignited against her neck. The fearsome wailing reverberated throughout the basement.

She pulled her brother close. He wore a terrified expression and held his hands over his ears. The sound rattled his teeth and stood his hairs on end even more than usual.

"It's *OK*," Diana said, as she urged him toward the stairs, her arms across his shoulders, her face registering none of the distress that the sound would afford any other human ear.

"Everything's OK, I promise," Diana soothed again. Limp with dread and still holding his ears, Brody followed her lead. Though his older sister's calm composure made no sense, he clung to it and to her.

The sound followed them to the top of the stairs. Linda Santos stood poised to enter the basement, her face contorted in worry at the bizarre clangor. Nicki and Jake had run into the room and stood just behind her, as she held her arms out to prevent either of them from proceeding toward Diana and the surreal and fearful sound.

But it raised no fear in Diana. No, quite the opposite. For though she had never heard it before, she knew—she felt—the incredible, fantastical sound of a dragon egg about to hatch.

Chapter Twelve

The Hatchings

"What is it, what is it?!" Brody was nearly hysterical. His cries were drowned out by the unearthly ringing from below. Dr. Kim closed the door behind them; even still, the sound was deafening.

Diana dragged her brother out of the kitchen and down to the end of the hall, everyone else following. It only added to Brody's agitation that her smile and bounce were so incongruent with the clamor. "I have to get back down there," Diana said urgently. "Don't worry. It's totally OK. In fact, I promise you, it's awesome!"

Nicki and Jake exchanged looks. They knew. They flanked Diana, forming a defensive line, putting themselves between the route to the basement and her little brother.

Brody's face was still screwed up in bewilderment; he kept his hands covering his ears, until his sister's next muffled, but intelligible, utterance got through to him: "It's OK! The dragon eggs are hatching!"

"What? No way!" Brody exclaimed, dropping his hands. He attempted to bolt toward the basement, but the three friends kept him from making any forward progress. He tried to squeeze through, crying, "The eggs are hatching? How cool!" Linda Santos took over, taking her son firmly by the hand.

Dr. Kim said, "This is extraordinary." Then she looked to little Brody and added, "But if I've learned one thing about nature, it's what constitutes a warning. And *that* sound certainly does."

Diana nodded, adding, "I can tell the mistcrystal is protecting me. I hear the sound, but it isn't scary or even that loud, really."

Brody tried to pull his mother toward the basement door. She stood firm. Dr. Kim was now rummaging through a disorganized plastic bin in the linen closet. "I've got earplugs in here, I know it." Her grown son was a drummer.

"We'll keep an eye on this guy," Jake said, and Nicki nodded, then got close to Brody and asked, "Do you really want to get closer to that noise?" Brody gave up his struggle, his hands flying back up over his ears against the auditory assault.

"You go," Linda said, smiling widely at her daughter. With that, Diana bounded back downstairs.

Brody had held his ears for good reason. The center harmonics of the *birth kelling*—indescribably sweet—were only for dragon ears. The rest of the strange sound was accounted for by a magical cacophony that essentially wrapped the beautiful kelling in caustic, otherworldly tones. In fact, it had the power to painfully ward off anyone but dragons, at least from the immediate vicinity of the nest, giving the parents a cocoon of sound within which to welcome their new young.

Diana had no need for auditory protection, however, because the mistcrystal channeled the birth kelling through its center, so the nucleus of the call became part of the crystal and, therefore, like a natural part of Diana. Its tenor resounded within her as a feeling of pure, joyful expectancy. If this was the effect on Diana, the dragon parents themselves must be euphoric.

Diana bent close to the nest. It pulsated with colored light. There was no danger from outside light now that the hatching was imminent, but the bright midday sunshine seemed amiss, so she left the draping pinned back halfway. She shone her elucifier at the nest and the patterns and hues of the eggs danced as if the colors themselves were three dimensional. It was the most beautiful sight she had ever seen.

Diana's face and body absorbed an increasing warmth as the heat from Clarin and Shay joined a growing heat from the eggs. The eggs gave off a unified pulse matched by Diana's mistcrystal. Diana was welcomed as a sort of hatching midwife, so she stayed close, an eager witness and willing helpmate.

Diana wished Nicki and Jake, and even her little brother, could witness the hatchings; but direct exposure to the birth kelling would permanently damage their hearing, if not their minds. They would have to be content with coming in after the hatchings were complete. She felt a pang. She wished her father could be here to see the arrival of the eleven baby dragons.

The thought reminded her of the twelfth. She glanced over at the slain little ghost egg, still so cold. Her heart sank at the perverse beauty of the pearlescent hull that no longer carried the life begun there. Hot tears rolled from her eyes. She shivered. Then, feeling the increasing heat from the beckoning new lives, she turned back to the nest, her teardrops dotting the dusty shelf between the dragon never-to-be and those about to be born.

Clarin and Shay leaned toward their eggs and Diana followed suit, giving the waiting parents only as much room as her excitement allowed. She gasped. *It was happening.* A tiny black claw protruded from a silvery egg. It pulled back its shell to reveal pale turquoise scales above the talon that directed its expedition into the new, wide world. The shell crackled and gave way just a fraction of an inch, where a light blue snout appeared to sniff at the outside air.

As the hatchling employed another claw in the task of self-birth, Diana caught sight of the eyes, half open but clear, and already a blaze of azure. The baby was nearly free of its shell, which fell in pieces around it. *The first one.* Diana let out her breath, only then realizing she had been holding it. She swayed at the wonder of it all, reaching for the ledge to steady herself.

Clarin and Shay reached out with their snouts and nudged their new baby. Its eyes opened wider, and it instinctively gripped a claw extended by each parent. Clarin quickly nuzzled the baby toward its father, who sat at the edge of the grassy nest, his body angled away from the other eggs. She then pushed the cast-off shell pieces behind the new dragonling. The baby *sea*, like its father, had a faint streak down its back in the shape of a long, stretchy "z." Now drawn under Shay's protective wings, the baby's light blue scales morphed into a radiant teal as the first peak of fire built up within the new dragon.

Shay touched snouts with his offspring and the first fire breath erupted from the dragonling: a diminutive aqua flame, but startling in its brightness. A hatchling's first breath, always one of fire, was what the dragons called the *bright kelling*.

As the baby sea sputtered out little blue flares, Shay positioned the shell fragments beneath the micro-explosions. Diana watched, eyes wide, taking in every motion and response between the dragon father and child. For all its exertion, Diana had to smile; the first fire breathing was completely adorable. The little blue-green creature, balancing itself on mouse-sized feet, coughed and spat in a struggle to inhale its first air, then continued its fledgling emissions. The flame steadied and narrowed to become a thin, cerulean stream. Meanwhile, the father and mother aimed their firebreaths in laser-like beams, searing the shells.

The parents added the eerie and beautiful strains of the *welcome kelling*, an inner song issuing directly from their heartfires, which swelled to a crescendo as the rays of heat melted the shells.

The baby dragon continued to follow its parents' example, its blue-green body alternately illumined or subdued with each gulping inhalation and fiery exhalation. The magic of the welcome kelling and the dragon family's communal firebreath reached a powerful finale that suspended the melted shells in the air before them and spun them into a sphere. When the object descended and cooled, the dragonling firmed up its soft new snout by tapping on the sphere until both were strong, solid, and shining.

Thus was formed the first new dragon's mistcrystal: a pale gem with the hatchling's first breath of seafoam vapor churning inside it like mist above waves. The new *sea* already had a name, known now only by Clarin and Shay. When the mistcrystal, with all those from the new hatchlings, was embedded permanently in the foundation of its home—wherever that may be now—the name would be given. When the parents' powers returned and Diana once again shared telepathy with Clarin, she would also receive the hatchlings' names.

The peculiar symphony of the first birth kelling faded to a close. Diana set her outstretched hand next to the little dragon. He or she—the gender would be claimed when the dragons were named—measured under four inches long. Its wings were nearly transparent, its body a shimmery sky blue. It hobbled on little blue-black feet, attempting to steady itself by gripping Diana's finger. Her mistcrystal hummed with the pulse of this new life, this new child of Clarin's, whose own first breath perpetually warmed Diana.

Before Diana could formulate a response to the miracle before her, the next birth kelling began to rise. In seconds it was at full pitch, and a second egg, a *sun*, displayed the tell-tale brilliance of imminent hatching.

From this peachy-red fireball poked one sharp talon, followed by a whole rosy-scaled foot. Immediately, the foot withdrew and the entire snout punched through the encasement, so the little orb rocked between the parents with the blushing ruby dragon's head protruding. The little sun pulled its head back into its shell, and two petite, blazing feet crushed the rest of the shell from within. The baby sun practically jumped out of its former home—landing atop the pile of fragments—and wobbled to a stand.

Diana smiled down at the salmon-colored creature that would become a passionate, crimson dragon in a few weeks. Right now, it looked like it belonged in her little brother's Easter basket.

Clarin and Shay hurried to position the child and the egg shards, for this dragon's bright kelling built inside it quickly, turning the pastel hatchling a searing blood-orange. It blew its first firebreath into the shell fragments with twice the heat as had the first-hatched sibling. The frill around the dragon baby's face shone a vibrant red, hinting at the sun's future magnificence.

The shells began to melt even before the adult dragons joined in with their fires. As the welcome kelling rose, the molten shell mass spun furiously, then came to a landing. The new mistcrystal took its hammered shape under the tappings of the baby, whose fiery face mirrored the swirling, scarlet breath sealed inside.

When the baby sun's welcome kelling subsided, Diana was forced to forego interacting with the second dragon child, for she heard shouts in the distance. She looked longingly at the hatching scene, gave Clarin and Shay as reassuring an expression as she could muster, and ran up to the kitchen.

Diana threw open the door and nearly knocked Nicki over. Nicki had on a pair of bulky black headphones and an audio recorder slung in front of her on a long strap. "Dr. Kim set me up," Nicki said way too loudly, but simultaneously pointed her anxious friend to the living room. "Look out the window," she added, again much louder than necessary. The noises seemed to be coming from the front yard, though they were quickly becoming obscured by the resonating birth kelling rising from below. She ran to the living room, also empty. Through the filmy drapery on the large front window she saw spinning red and blue lights. *What the heck?* She pushed aside one corner of the curtain and looked out. Jake was on the porch, his back to the house. He stood at attention, a strong but skinny sapling of a bodyguard. Diana ran to the door, cracked it open, and hissed, "Jake!"

Jake turned just enough to flash a quick smile at his friend, shouting, "Don't worry, my dad's got it!" He resumed his posture with his back to her and his eyes on the crowd of people on the lawn.

"Oh, geez, thank God. Those are *his* lights," Diana said, relieved. Sheriff Gonzales's car was parked at the end of the driveway, lights blazing. He was out of the car, standing in the middle of the yard, talking to a young woman in a dark skirt and blazer. He was gesticulating toward the driveway where a white van idled. A huge antenna appeared to be growing out of the roof like a lifeless magic beanstalk. The side of the van read "Channel 8 News" in blue and white.

Diana stared at Jake, her jaw gaping. "Dr. Kim called my dad," Jake continued, shouting over his shoulder. "She knew the noise would freak out the neighbors. Dang, she was not kidding."

"Yeah, and it's going to go on for nine more hatchings," Diana replied. At that, Jake chanced another quick look at Diana, excitement lighting up his features. Diana rewarded him by going on, "We've already got a sea and a sun! They're amazing."

"Cool!" Jake exclaimed.

Diana took one more visual sweep of the chaos outside while calling to Jake, "I better get back down there." Her ears had already trained to another welcome kelling. The next hatchling had to be out of its shell. She dashed into the kitchen. Nicki was back up against the basement door with the microphone, waving it around like the toy "tricorder" she had when they were younger. She blushed slightly and paused to pull the door open for Diana, then closed it quickly and quietly behind her.

A little sun stood between its parents. This one had a funny, spiky frill and two squiggly lines running down the sides of its face. It would have looked fierce had it not looked so cute. She watched as the mistcrystal spun and landed, and the new sun began its instinctual hammering on the gem that held its precious breath. It crawled behind the nest of siblings-to-be to join the other two hatchlings. The three snuggled beneath Clarin in a heap of rassling violet.

Another sun arrived next, then still another. *I guess they're on the same wavelength*, Diana joked to herself, feeling giddy. She relished each stage of the hatching and mistcrystal rituals. She loved watching the differences in their first fire-breathing attempts, as well as seeing the shadowy indicators of each dragonling's distinctive markings, all of which would darken over the next few weeks.

The single caramel-colored egg began to fluoresce. The egg resembled abundant gold ore in a bed of sandstone. The energy in Diana's mistcrystal felt as if it matched the pulse of this egg exactly. The sixth hatchling: it was the *terra*. The egg sparkled so brightly, and the efficient claw was followed so quickly by the sienna snout and front legs, that Diana barely saw the shell crack and fall away. It formed something of a clam-like bottom shell, as the wide-eyed terra stood straight up on the opened half, a miniature dragon Venus.

It took its parents' claws so surely, it was hard to believe it had hatched just moments before.

The beauty of the terra's first firebreath took Diana's own breath away. A fervent amber flame licked the two pieces of shell until they collapsed into a honeyed mass containing flecks of shining, untold minerals. Clarin and Shay added their welcome kelling. Clarin's firebreath shone like pure gold, a grander reproduction of their offspring's modest yet unfaltering flame.

Diana sighed at the sight of the cooling mistcrystal. Almost identical to her own, the new terra's mistcrystal seemed to unite with hers, humming and swirling, pulling Diana toward the dragonling. She opened her palm in front of the golden-brown being, dragon parents regarding them beneficently. She tried to keep herself from trembling as it climbed determinedly into her hand.

The four-inch long terra attempted to spread its wings, its gilded face tilted toward Diana's. As it stretched the gauzy wings, it fell forward and smashed its stubby snout into Diana's palm. Laughing, Diana gingerly gripped the baby and righted it, leaning her face close in. "Nice try. Even a terra needs a minute to adjust to life in the big wide world." The terra looked intensely into Diana's eyes. "I think you already understand me, don't you?" Diana murmured, as the tiny dragon—by all clues a mini Clarin—showed its gift for understanding by sitting on its haunches and nestling into the curve of Diana's hand. Time stopped. This life imprinted on her and she on it. Diana stared, stroked the warm little back, and cupped her other hand loosely around her new friend, absorbing the warmth and the beating heart in sync with the pulse on her own throat.

A gentle nip from Shay brought Diana back from her world of two. She let the terra hop onto the ledge and scoot back to its mother, where, under Clarin's nuzzles and coos, it joined the jostling rainbow brood.

Diana's attention was rerouted at the sound of the next birth kelling. This was the *ghost*, the one who had survived the dark kelling. Diana saw the clear claw tear its way through the fragile shell, her heart a teeter-totter of heaviness and happiness. She couldn't help feeling as if the new baby had lost its twin. It really didn't work that way with dragons—they were all siblings equally—but the loss of the other ghost permeated her, a layer of gloom threatening to mute the arrival of this single, pale hatchling. When it pushed its opalescent snout through the blanched shell, Diana's elation resurfaced.

The ghost dragonling freed itself completely from its constraints. The strands of straw on the ledge showed murkily through the ghost's frame, as if the hatchling was made of tiny, wheat-colored spears. As Clarin and Shay moved through the rituals with their infant ghost, their communal firebreath transformed its insubstantial, delicate shell into a kernel resembling highly glossed mother-of-pearl. The mistcrystal glowed with an ethereal luminescence. Diana felt she might levitate along with the new dragonling's mistcrystal, though she also picked up on the dragon parents' heightened protectiveness toward their most vulnerable new child.

The ghost was number seven. Four eggs pulsated in the straw between Clarin and Shay. The birth kelling for another hatchling began. Before she could look to see which of the four remaining dragons was preparing to emerge, loud shouts once again reached her from outside. One voice was much louder than any she'd heard previously.

"Everyone please stay back...*under penalty of trespassing!*"

Diana ran upstairs and looked out the living room window. Sheriff Gonzales held an electric megaphone. Jake was still standing on the porch, though now he leaned on the railing of the front steps. Also on the porch stood Sheriff Gonzales's most trusted deputy, Laura Sullivan, her back to the house and arms folded. Diana cracked the door. To her shock, she saw cars lining the road and a cluster of onlookers—a few at the end of the driveway, some on the lawn. Deputy Sullivan repeated the order for everyone to stay away from the house. When the last onlooker retreated to at least the edge of the property, Sheriff Gonzales spoke again, "There is no danger. Everything is under control."

The small crowd all talked at once. A woman in a long, beige sweater shouted over everyone, "No danger, Sheriff? Then what's all that noise?" She pulled her sweater more tightly around her.

A man in jeans and a t-shirt chimed in, "Yeah, really, Sheriff. We're going to take your word for it? It sounds like cats are being tortured in there."

Dr. Kim was over to the left side of the porch, talking to the reporter. Diana caught the reporter's eager eye and slammed the front door, not that Dr. Kim would ever have allowed her in.

Diana heard Dr. Kim's voice over the megaphone. "We promise a full report in due time. We are experiencing a rare zoological event."

Now it was the Sheriff speaking again. "I assure you, once more, there is no danger. Please bear with us. Thank you."

Before closing the door, Diana had spied her mom walking around, Brody in tow, making sure no one disobeyed the instructions to stay away. Diana headed back to the basement, marveling quietly to herself, *Wow: a news truck, police lights, strangers in the yard—just like in the movies.* She almost started to laugh, but shivered instead.

By the time Diana got back to the nest, a new sea had finished its entry into the world. She observed with continued wonder and satisfaction as the last two seas arrived.

Finally, through a jubilant smile, she sighed, "You're the last one..." as the eleventh dragonling, a sun, arrived and completed its birth kelling.

They were all here, all healthy, and all climbing over one another. The mistcrystals were pushed into the center of the brood and the proud parents were nudging each baby and beaming at their creations. Diana watched in awe, putting her hand into the pile of dragonlings and laughing as their harmless firebreath warmed her skin. At a sudden burning sensation, she whipped her hand back, observing where one of the little suns had singed the hairs on her arm. She laughed even harder, regarding the scorching as a badge of honor. "Control your babies," she said, returning the grins of the parents.

Chapter Thirteen

The Death Kelling

Diana looked at the dragon family, the
hatchlings instinctively arranged around their
mistcrystals, their inner fire and the vibrations
from the crystals synchronized and stunning.

"I guess the namings are next, huh?" Diana
chirped. Then, as she followed the new parents'
eyes, she shuddered and wrapped her arms
around herself. They all looked reverently
toward the edge of the nest. A stillness settled
among them like Diana had never felt.

"Oh." Her voice fell. "Is it now?" The
dragons nodded, their bodies drawn close to
the teeming brood and mistcrystals. Clarin
guided Diana's eyes toward the stairs.

Clarin and Shay settled over their nest and
began to pull from the store of worms that
Diana had ready for them. While they fed their
hatchlings, Diana had a few minutes. She
watched for a few moments as the beautiful
new lives adorably and awkwardly gobbled up
the sustenance, then walked quickly up the
stairs. With each step, her heart felt like a hot

air balloon trying to rise while still weighted to stay aground.

She would see who could get away from the chaos outside. They were going to meet eleven baby dragons, and say goodbye to one who never got to be.

Diana went back to the front door and opened it wide enough to see the news van packing up.

"What happened?" she called to Jake.

"Dr. Kim and my dad talked to the reporter."

"They told?" she gasped, one hand flying to her mistcrystal.

"Don't worry. They made up some story about falcons with a rare disease."

Diana met this with a dubious look.

"Yeah, I know...lame," Jake continued. "They didn't really buy it. But then my dad threatened to arrest them for trespassing if they set one toe on the property. It was awesome."

Sheriff Gonzales walked up and interjected, "I was starting to wonder if they were really going to leave. I would have had to make good on my threat and arrest the T.V. crew." He rubbed his chin and semi-chuckled. "But then who would report it on the 11 o'clock news?"

158

He directed himself at Diana alone. "How is it with the little ones?" he asked with an expectant smile.

The wonder of it all flashed before her eyes. "They're great," she said, "but—" She cast her eyes down. The Sheriff put a hand on her shoulder. She looked up, her face somber. Then she looked at Jake.

"Can you go get everyone?" Her voice was small, quiet. Jake regarded her with intensity as she went on. "They're going to perform the death kelling for the little ghost."

At this the sheriff sighed deeply, as Jake replied,"Oh, wow, yeah," his voice suddenly mature, compassionate. "I'll get them." Jake went off to perform his duty.

Diana looked at his profile for a moment before she addressed Jake's dad, "Can you still keep watch?"

"Of course, kiddo," the sheriff said.

Diana went back to the basement. Everyone was there in a matter of moments. Linda Santos stood with Brody in front of her.

"Look at the baby dragons!" Brody exclaimed. His mother put her hand on Brody's shoulder and whispered something in his ear. His eyes roved to the ghost egg. "Oh, no. I forgot," he said. He stared at the egg and choked out a little sob that made him sound much younger. This brought up the tears that were just below the surface for everyone else.

In a way, they had all lived with the dragonkin—invested their hopes and desires and love, in their unseen, magical family—for the past two years. Such a loss was a blow they could never have anticipated. Diana, Jake, and Nicki exchanged looks, Jake not bothering to hide his tears, which welled in his eyes like a creek about to spill over its banks. Diana's streamed down each cheek in a single line and fell to the floor.

As if on cue, everyone moved in closer around Diana, who stood directly in front of Clarin and Shay. They had herded the little brood into the straw behind them.

Heat drained from the dragon parents. Their living children became still, their bodies taking on much dimmer shades, but their tiny heartfires each glowing softly. They lay in various attitudes, snouts toward their cooling parents.

Outside of death, dragons never become colder than when mourning a child. Clarin and Shay's scales lost all luminescence, as if each wore a cloak made of fog. Shay picked up the broken egg in his mouth and placed it gently between him and Clarin. They looked down together at the torn shell. The ghostly white orb was split nearly in two, the jagged aftermath of the dark kelling. Once the outside air had touched the unborn dragon, it froze, to remain suspended in icebound sorrow until the death kelling occurred.

Diana's mistcrystal now felt like ice; the breath inside was still. Diana dropped to her knees, no notice of the bits of cement dust digging into her skin. Her eyes were now level with the little ghost egg. Shay covered Clarin's right fore-talon with his left. Together they raised their claws to hover millimeters over the egg, their movements creating a wave of frost that clung to the surface of the shell. They moved in unison until the icy coating was complete.

The dragon parents encircled the egg with their joined claws. They clamped their eyes shut. A call, quiet at first, like the cry of a mourning dove, but drawn out, as if pulled slowly and deliberately from the creature's hearts, grew to permeate the still, cold air. This was the *grief kelling*: a forlorn, melodious whine; a low, musical moaning that reverberated with loss.

In a sudden flash, the mistcrystal and parent dragons' heartfires burst with light and heat. Then, just as quickly, the mournful frigidity returned. In that moment, characters appeared on the eggshell, etched magically in the frost. Diana's mistcrystal translated the dragon-glyphs before her eyes into the baby's name. She took a deep breath, determined not to cry. She cupped her hands loosely around the egg, not touching it, but letting the cold saturate her palms. She put her hands to her mouth and let the name escape her lips like steam:

"*P h a e d.*"

The name brushed everyone's ears like the breath the dragon never took. At the sound of it, Clarin and Shay put their faces to the egg and closed their eyes. They inhaled deeply until a dusting of frost began to cover their faces, then slowly crept over their whole bodies. The basement was cold. This time Diana knew it was not just her. Involuntary shivers ran through everyone, but not even little Brody complained.

Clarin and Shay were completely draped in blankets of frost. They both held their breath.

They were as still as death, and now nearly prostrate before their dead child. Diana held her mistcrystal away from her body. It felt frozen; the opaque mist looked like a winter lake. She found herself holding her breath as well. The dragons and egg formed a kind of sculpture, a trio of snowy death.

The brood of hatchlings looked even more muted, their tiny heartfires like colored lanterns in a window across a rainy street. Just as a prickling fear began to crawl up Diana's spine, both parents opened their eyes wide. Clarin's irises were blazing white rings, and Shay's, torrential crashing waves. They inhaled deeply for what seemed like minutes. Then, with their eerie, arctic gazes locked on the egg, they aimed their concentrated exhalations at the shell. The breath, a freezing mist changing to an opaque, flowing fog, caused the name to evaporate before enveloping the lost egg in a billowing gray cloud. At this, Diana repeated quietly, reverently, "Phaed." As if directed, the rest of the human voices in the room whispered the name in unison: *"Phaed."*

Chapter Fourteen

Phaed's Shiftcrystal

Clarin and Shay remained crouched before the egg they mourned, the name hanging in the air like the cold. Shay lifted himself on weary forewings and lay close to his mate's side. They opened their mouths, each barely moving, and emitted a hissing steam that joined in the air in front of them before landing on the egg. When their combined breath touched the egg, it changed to a yellow flame. Widening, the fire turned from yellow to red to blue. All was absorbed by the egg that would have been Phaed.

In a flash, the parents' blue firebreath exploded into a blinding white fireball. Phaed's broken shell was completely incinerated, and its remains imploded with a loud crack leaving only a mound of sparkling white flecks. Diana thought, *If snowflakes could burn...*

While watching the ritual, Diana's mistcrystal changed from cold to hot and back to cold. Inside, it mirrored Phaed's flurry of flames and fragments. Diana's shoulders heaved in silent sobs.

Tears flowed freely from everyone else, too. The burst of the fragile shell—the fragments of un-lived life—reflected in their sodden, shining eyes like individual snowstorms. Each of their faces absorbed the radiance of Phaed's last moment of solidity on this earth.

The dragon parents continued their firebreathing, every inch of them seeming to feed what was to come next: the *burial kelling*. In another flash, they scorched the tiny hill of crystal flecks into a sphere: a dazzling, melting diamond. The two dragons raised their heads a fraction of an inch, and the mass spun faster and faster between them until it was perfectly round. The dragons' breath reversed in sequence from white-hot to yellow fire, to steam, and finally, back to frost. Clarin and Shay dropped their heads and appeared to breathe normally again. Diana put a hand on each dragon's back. Their temperatures must have matched the air, because she detected almost nothing. Her mistcrystal felt invisible on her throat, tepid and still, like the dragons.

The cooled crystal had settled onto the nest of straw. The crystal's pristine ghost-dragon hues were interrupted by one jagged, blood-red line all the way through the center. Phaed's shiftcrystal was born. And soon it must be buried.

Chapter Fifteen

The Suggestion of Sacrifice

The plate glass window shattered under the force of electric blasts. The sheer lavender curtains ignited, melting and curling at the singed edges. Diana shot up from where she slept on the couch, sparks landing on her blanket and in her hair. Her arms flew up to protect her face and head, and another bolt of electric power struck the cut on her arm. The shining white scar sizzled where Ayan had scratched her. A shock ran up her arm; her mistcrystal sizzled and stung her throat.

The nearly transparent dragon flew at her, pinning her to the couch, his furious wings flapping, blocking her movements to either side. With one hand she tried to lift the burning mistcrystal off her flesh; the other flailed at the hovering marauder. Spurs of lightning zapped her arms and legs. Diana saw a dreadful inferno fill the body of the enraged ghost as it pulled back and inhaled, teeth bared, ready to hurl a final incinerating blast.

"Ayan! Ayan, no!" Diana's pleas were drowned out by the gathering crackle of electricity. He opened his jaws. She screamed, "No-o-o—!"

They all heard her screams. Jake, just arriving and crossing the yard, broke into a run toward the house and scaled the four front stairs in one bound. Maddened by the locked front door, he rattled the knob, pounding and shouting, peering into the narrow glass inset.

Diana sat bolt upright on the couch, perspiration on her forehead, breath heaving. Dr. Kim ran in from the kitchen with Nicki on her heels. She gestured to the door where Nicki unbolted the lock, to be nearly thrown aside as Jake pushed open the door. Dr. Kim sat next to Diana, her arm around her. Nicki stood before her friend, eyes searching everywhere around the room for clues to the disturbance. Jake's eyes darted around the room as he ran to the hallway, then to the kitchen, where he rattled the back door lock, then returned to the living room. "What's wrong? What happened?" he asked.

"Ayan blew up the window with his firecurrent. He threw himself at me over and over," Diana choked out, gasping, while running her hands over her arms, looking for the burn marks that had felt so real moments ago. They all looked from Diana to the plate glass, which was fully intact.

"He flew over me, trapped me," she said as she swung her legs off the couch. "His firecurrent kept burning me; it went through my mistcrystal and burned my throat."

Jake sat down close to Diana, while Nicki took a place next to him.

"It's okay. It was just a nightmare," Nicki said, though she looked around the room again. Dr. Kim echoed the soothing words. Diana's shoulders dropped. She sank into the couch, leaning on Jake the slightest bit, a sigh of relief coming from her lips.

Jake stood up. "Want some water?" Before she could reply, he ran to the kitchen and returned with a cup.

"Thanks." Diana gulped down the water and handed Jake the empty cup. Her companions regarded her quietly. "I'm fine." A dawning look came over her. She stood, throwing off the blanket, knees wobbling for just a moment, and looked at the three whose faces were turning from worry to interest.

"Before Ayan attacked, I saw something else in my dream. We have more clues than we thought. I need the journals." She looked at her phone. Dead.

"I've got it," Nicki said, pulling out her phone and texting Mrs. Santos. The phone dinged in moments. "Your mom wants to know which ones."

"The first three. No, five, to be safe," Diana answered, sitting back down next to Jake. Dr. Kim was back in the kitchen, calling them to come and eat something.

Nicki sent the text. "You figured out a ton those first few days."

"*We* did," Diana corrected her.

Almost every day after school, and on weekends and holidays—for hours on end—Diana and Nicki had holed up in the room, Diana quoting everything she heard from the missive on the wall, Nicki taking it down in the journals. Jake had joined in whenever his dad could drive him over, though Nicki rarely let Jake do any of the transcribing.

Diana's mother had made a sturdy leather and wire necklace for the mistcrystal. Before putting it on, Diana had let Jake and Nicki try holding the magical charm up to the wall. Nothing happened. Apparently this was somewhat to Nicki's relief, considering the eagerness with which she had returned the gem to her friend's custody. Jake tried a couple more times, then gave up. After that, Diana had never removed the necklace.

Before the missive, Diana and Nicki—best friends and neighbors since first grade—had played endlessly at the fantasy games their imaginations created. They transformed themselves into horses, unicorns, wizards, royalty. Diana usually led them to some adventure in the rainforest. Incorporating what her father had told her, she turned stories of his work into mystical plots and settings even more lush than those her father described.

Then, suddenly, they had actual fantastic creatures to learn about through real, live magic. They put all their childhood energy and wonder into their new reality and into unlocking the mysteries that, by examining every nuance of the missive, could tame—at least on Diana's better days—some of the ache of missing her father.

"Remember when we used to pretend we were explorers?" Diana said to Nicki, none of the fun from their prior imaginings making it into her voice.

"And we would be attacked by gorillas throwing flaming coconuts?" Nicki managed a weak laugh as she finished the recollection. She turned wistful, "Then you got a dragon—"

Diana snapped back to the present moment. "How are the dragons?" Her eight hours of sleep suddenly seemed like weeks away from the dragon family.

"I just checked on them," Nicki said, nodding toward the basement. "The dragonlings are unbelievably cute. The suns look like little 'peeps'!" Everyone smiled. Diana was already on her way out of the room. "But," Nicki added, "Clarin seemed a little agitated."

"Maybe it was all those babies bugging her," Jake said, following Diana. Nicki, right behind, paused to ask Dr. Kim if she needed help, to which Dr. Kim replied with a shooing motion, nudging Nicki away from the food preparation and toward the basement door.

Any residual dread from Diana's nightmare dissolved at the sight of the nest of dragonlings. Gold, blue, red, and pearl, they climbed all over one another. A few worms and pre-chewed bits of fruit lay at the side of their cement playground.

Diana, Nicki, and Jake pulled up old stools that sat about the dark basement. Diana had the 'luce shining, but asked the parents if daylight was welcome. They nodded their assent, so Jake went over and pulled at the draping, upsetting a few nails as he tugged, and let it hang down sloppily. He ran the rest of the way up the stairs and threw open the door to the kitchen, calling, "They want light!" and then ran back down.

"I'll put the cat out," Dr. Kim called cheerfully.

"Look at them!" Diana said, smiling and pointing to the five little seas who circled together, their heartfires pulsating in unison while they breathed into the center of the circle, and then hopped around while the diffuse and harmless embers danced near one another's feet. The four suns pushed at the circle to join as Shay pushed away more straw, creating a miniature arena. The suns, red hearts beating in sync, aimed fire into the circle, creating violet infusions with their siblings' aquamarine breaths.

Diana tickled the little ghost, who responded with tumbles over her extended hand. Jake joined in, while Nicki put off the interactions in favor of recording them on her cell phone.

The dragonlings performed a clumsy circus of somersaults and levitations on wings looking like cotton candy stretched over toothpicks. Flapping as rapidly as they could, they rose only inches above their playmates' hands and one another. The ghost, whose front chest plate bore a light, almost transparent circle, fell off Diana's hand, just inches from the ledge, landing in a belly flop. "Is it OK?" Nicki asked, setting aside the video recording. The little ghost stood, stuck its snout bravely into the air, and shook like a wet puppy, which only sent it tumbling again. The friends laughed.

The little terra, who sat regally on its own, shaped its breath into an amber stream, small but bright, which it aimed at a scale shed by Shay, causing a miniscule searing. At that, its breath turned to smoke, landing on the scale and floating over and around it in a pillow of taupe. The baby ghost watched, rapt, though it could not yet have understood it was witnessing the terra's firebreath adaptation powers already emerging.

Diana looked at Clarin, about to say something about the new terra child. The mini Clarin had enveloped itself in smoky haze. Diana's mistcrystal thrummed. But the words on the tip of her tongue vanished, as Diana was shocked to hear instead: *Diana. We must—*

"What?" she said aloud, sounding oddly agitated. She received an inquiring look from Jake and another pause in video recording from Nicki. *Clarin?!* She thought. She had heard her voice—Clarin's voice—inside her head. It was hushed, almost weak, but she knew she had heard it. She stared at Clarin, who nodded. Shay reached behind the new terra, drawing Diana's attention back to the little terra's play. "Of course. Your little ones are starting to get their powers, so you're both getting yours back, too?" she asked aloud.

At that, Jake was drawn to the baby terra's hazy scene, while Nicki clicked the video recorder back on and zoomed in. "Wow!" Jake exclaimed. "What's going on?"

Repeating it as she heard it in her mind from Clarin, Diana explained the magical adaptation to the firebreath of the terra: its power to make "smokeless smoke." "They call it the *firefog*."

"Cool," said Jake. "But I'd call it fire*smog*."

Diana chuckled. Nicki put her nose into the firefog and breathed deeply. "It appears to have no properties of smoke other than visual: no smell, no toxins." The baby terra blew another puff into Nicki's face, at which Diana and Jake cracked up.

Diana straightened her face and continued, "The other hatchlings will get their extra powers, soon, too." She paused, then added,

"And Clarin says you're right: no toxins. In fact, it's good for you."

Nicki gave Jake a satisfied smirk. "Wait, what are you looking at me for?" he asked.

"Habit, I guess," Nicky said. They all laughed again.

Nicki got back to the subject. "So the parents' magic will be back soon," she stated, the lessons from the missive coming back to her easily. She flipped the camera back on and started recording again. She aimed the camera at Diana, who now had the terra hatchling on her forearm like a falcon, the dragon blowing firefog toward the lens like a special effect.

"I almost feel guilty enjoying these little guys, with their sisters and brothers still missing," Diana said. Her thoughts were interrupted by Clarin's patchy telepathy trying to tell her something. Diana waved off Nicki, who clicked off the recording.

Diana moved in front of Clarin. "What's up?" she asked, speaking aloud to include the other humans. Before Clarin could respond, they heard the door open and close upstairs. Diana's mom was here. "My journals!" Diana exclaimed. "Clarin, the four symbols...the circle in the center...I've seen them before, haven't I?"

The dragon nodded, solemn, eyes fixed on Diana. The mistcrystal hummed again. *Yes, go look.* The dragon's frazzled but lyrical thoughts coursed through Diana. She flew to the stairs. "Hurry up, you two..." But they were already right behind her.

Diana ran straight through the kitchen as Dr. Kim called after her, "Eat!"

"I will in a minute!" She was too worked up.

"Mom!" Diana called out. In the living room, Mrs. Santos, Brody in tow, had the journals out on the coffee table and was staving off the boy's curious hands. Nicki, who had written as much as Diana, grabbed one and held it open in her lap.

"The *ouroboros*. It's in here, like we remembered," Nicki said.

"Ouro...what?" Jake said, almost remembering it right, himself.

"Ouroboros," Dr. Kim finished the strange word. "The dragon swallowing its tail, a symbol of several things—some ominous, such as immortality."

"Yeah, that," Jake said. "And it's not good. That's what was on Illsworth's weird vulture controls, right?" Diana nodded but kept leafing through the journals.

"Hey, you guys," Diana said, "do you remember that time the symbols on my wall kept glowing in a certain order—the same way, over and over? And as I touched each one, it changed and got all glittery and gold, and I heard a new word?" Diana leafed through the oldest journal as she spoke.

"Yes! That was the coolest day ever deciphering the missive." Jake was nodding. But then the rest of the memory hit Nicki. She continued ruefully, "The last one. It turned black. And gave you chills."

At this, Linda Santos quietly implored, "Diana?"

But her daughter wasn't listening.

What were the words again? What must they do? Diana continued to pour over the journal, while the rest sat in silence. She stopped on a page, read and reread it, then sat down, placed the journal on the table, and stabbed her finger onto the open page. "There." They all leaned in, barely a breath among them, staring at a depiction of the arrangement of symbols Clarin had scratched out by the nest. Then, soberly, Diana said the words: "The QuinKell."

More silence. Even Brody stood quietly, absorbing the somber mood. Nicki took the journal from her friend and stared at the page. Jake looked over her shoulder. "This symbol...it stands for four dragons, one of each nature..." Nicki said. Everyone hung on her explanation. She paused, looking at her friend, the color draining from her face. "The one below...it means sacrifice." Nicki said, and shivered. The silence was complete now. "And the one in the middle..."

"Yeah," Diana said, her voice dark and steely, "it's me."

Chapter Sixteen

The Dark Light

Everyone stared at Diana. Brody went to her side and took her hand, something he hadn't done voluntarily since he was five. Diana squeezed it . She shook her head and shoulders and smiled. "It's going to be OK." The first to look convinced was Jake, next Dr. Kim. Brody tugged at her. She looked down at her brother. "It's magic. It's gonna be OK," she said to his open little face. Their mother nodded and smiled, somewhat believably.

Diana reached for her throat. They all noticed the extra glow in her mistcrystal. "Your 'bat signal,'" Nicki said. That got a little laugh, and the tension lessened. Diana headed toward the basement, resigning on the way to keep Brody, whose hand still clung to hers, with her. Her mom made a move toward Brody, but Diana gave the big-sister-*It's-OK* look.

"Come up and eat soon," Dr. Kim said. "And we'll get more dragon food ready to take down."

In the kitchen, the others burst into activity and chatter, relieved to feel some semblance of a normal daily routine. Sheriff Gonzales texted Jake that he was on his way over.

"I'll double the coffee," Dr. Kim said, with a wink.

"Am I too young to start drinking it?" Nicki said, only half joking. "Maybe it would help me figure some things out." She had a journal in one hand.

"Why don't you relax awhile, Nicki?" said Mrs. Santos, gently taking the volume and setting it aside.

"And you can start drinking coffee anytime you want," Dr. Kim chided, "as long as it's in college, under your parents' watch, or *never*." Laughter filled the room.

Diana led Brody to the nest. He pulled away from her to stand across from the dragonlings, his head jutting out over the ledge, practically joining the brood. Diana was right beside him, and automatically guided his hand back when he made a move to reach for the little sun who had ventured to stand an inch from Brody's grin.

"Ok, I won't touch." Diana believed her brother's intentions, but pulled a stool over, helped him up on it, and stood with one leg partly in front of it, providing a distance she deemed safe while she concentrated on Clarin. She glanced at Shay knowingly, seeing that his attention was riveted upon the interactions of the boy and baby dragons. The little sun spat out a sparkler-strength fireball that landed on the shelf. Brody laughed and waited for the next. A sea was waddling toward its sibling to join in the fun with this new, giant, apple-faced friend.

Clarin and Diana stood inches apart. Inside her mind, Diana heard Clarin's voice, at first as if she were far away, then refined slowly, musically, until she heard in a clear, strong tone: *Diana.*

She answered silently: *Clarin.*

Diana. Bearer of my first breath. The words were faint but clear. At these words, the mistcrystal seemed to sing, insistent, yet soothing, a melody of warmth. *Wearer of the mistcrystal.* Their exchange brought a tear to Diana's eye. Diana stood tall, absorbing the calling. Though a single, cool thread of darkness and fear curled up inside the otherwise expansive feeling.

I know. The QuinKell, Diana thought.

Yes. We must summon the QuinKell. But first, my other children. We must free my other children.

At this, Clarin looked at Shay, who was peering over, clearly invited to track Clarin's communications to Diana.

My beloved mate will protect these, our new children. She looked tenderly at her young. *And we will free their sisters and brothers.*

If they're all alive, Diana tried to stop the thought, but it was too late. Shame rose within her.

Do not worry. My powers trickle steadily back. And I can feel— A powerful feeling of hope and joy came from Clarin just before the next words appeared in Diana's mind: *I feel their heartfires—the heartfires of all five.*

At this, Diana nearly seized the fragile dragon. Instead, she said aloud, "They're all alive!"

Brody startled and looked at his big sister. She grabbed him and hugged him hard. "Who's alive?" he began, then, awareness beyond his years filling in the blanks, he grabbed his sister and said, "The missing dragons? They're alive!" He jumped from the stool. "Can I, please—"

"Yeah, yeah, go on. Tell them!" Diana commissioned him to bear the news like a queen commissioning a knight. Brody took another look at the brand new dragons, beaming, and ran up the stairs, shouting, "You guys! You guys!..."

Diana turned back to Clarin. The dragon looked so tired. *Food. I'll be right back,* Diana thought. Clarin nodded. Diana dashed upstairs, parting the waves of joy that filled the air in the bright kitchen as they all basked in Brody's tidings. She managed to convey the request for sustenance amidst the grateful choruses and jostling hugs. "We'll be right down," Nicki and Jake said together.

"We'll take a peek, too, if that's all right," Dr. Kim said as she tossed her head to indicate Linda, "when the Sheriff gets here." Dr. Kim winked. Diana slipped back to the basement.

~

Diana and Clarin soared through the canyon, the wings of Diana's golden elementor bearing her surely beside the dragon. They dipped low over the scrub oaks, following the contours of the trickling creek, then rose above the tall, sparse live oaks to fly more slowly around the dense grove of avocado trees. At this point, Diana felt herself guided to follow closely behind Clarin. They followed the stand of dark green trees, staying just below the canopy to retain their cover.

Clarin rounded the last edge of the avocado grove before the mansion would be visible and flew to a camouflaging branch. Diana set down in the large branch beside her, concentrating on letting Clarin's telepathic navigation to guide her. As she touched down, she relinquished the connection too abruptly and swayed to a tenuous hold on the branch. *I could really use some claws for this part,* she thought.

Clarin, amused, responded, *Allow my energy to buoy you.*

Suddenly, it was as if Diana's high-tops had grown talons, and she clung assuredly to the living balance beam, her poise emulating that of the dragon.

The shiftcrystal. If he has left it here, we may be fortunate enough to go into the kelling dimension, Clarin thought, *though we may then have to deal with another vulture attack.*

Diana could not imagine Illsworth parting with the stolen magic. *Right*, she returned, *and any other nasty tricks he has up his sleeve.*

They had waited for a report from Sheriff Gonzales that Illsworth had gone into town. He would signal them and the others when Illsworth looked to be heading home. At Dr. Kim's house, Deputy Laura Sullivan stood guard, while Shay tended the hatchlings. Shay's returning telepathy, as well as his other powers, were not strong enough for such a distance, so communication with his mate was impossible for the time being.

Are you prepared? Clarin asked her young shadow.

Yes, Diana answered, wondering if her thoughts could sound as shaky as her voice would have.

All will go well. Follow me.

With a nod, they were again in flight, Diana's elementor popping open to full span the second her feet pushed off from the branch. They sailed high, nearly vertical for many yards, and over the iron fence to avoid the recently extended electronic triggers. Once Clarin detected electrically neutral air, she led Diana over, and the two flyers, wings in unison, came to rest on the rooftop of the mansion.

They perched at the edge of what appeared to be a skylight the size of patio doors, the same place from which the vultures had emerged days before.

Keep watch as I try to solder these doors closed, thought Clarin. Clarin aimed for a wide, metal strip where the doors met in the center of the huge skylight. As soon as she released the first scorching breath, a din rose from below. Diana looked through the heavy glass to see the room full of captive vultures, all bearing the odd control devices, teeming and screeching toward the transparent ceiling. Some flapped their wings in agitation, ineffectual either because they had no room to fly, or they had not been commanded to do so.

Let's go, they're too loud, Diana thought. They abandoned their efforts on the doors and flew down and around the house. As they alighted next to a side door, Diana thought, *What about his creepy employees?* Illsworth didn't have the typical staff for a property like this: gardeners, housekeepers, a "pool guy." He had a few heavy-booted, olive-shirted thugs who kept guard on the place. No one knew how many. They had received information from Sheriff Gonzales that two of them were in town with Illsworth.

Clarin's intuition told her there were no people in the immediate vicinity, but she barely trusted her so recently re-emerging powers. If only a *sun* were with them; they had the ability to detect any being's heartfire, even that of a cold-hearted goon.

Two huge, black dogs ran around the house, hurtling flat-out, jaws open. Clarin started, obviously surprised she had not felt their presence at least fleetingly. Diana stood in front of Clarin to face the dogs. The first set of giant black paws was upon her. She squealed, "Clarin, go!" as she was pushed to the ground.

Clarin flew to perch atop a miniature palm a few feet away. Diana lay beneath the 150-pound canine, its front feet pinning her, while her hands pushed against the massive chest. She shook her head to avoid the saliva that dripped from gleaming fangs as the beast covered Diana's cheeks with sloppy licks and nuzzles. The other ferocious creature paced and jumped at the foot of the palm, trying to reach the dragon to bestow similar greetings.

Clarin cooed soothingly—a dragon's birdsong—and the pit bull jumped off of Diana. The other one relaxed and reduced its pacing, giving Clarin the confidence to descend from the tree, knowing her eagle-sized frame would not be crushed under the happy exuberance of the dogs.

Diana petted the first dog, looking at its tag that said, *Shark*. "Here, boy," she called to the other, whose friendly nips still threatened to push Clarin off balance. She bent to read its name: *Alcatraz*. The names certainly hinted at how these dogs were trained to deal with intruders, let alone a dragon or a human they instinctively identified as one.

Clarin had no idea what the second name implied, but she read Diana's reaction well enough. *Poor things. I think we might come back for them another time.*

Diana stroked the two pooches for a few more seconds, then stood and shook out her elementor so it cascaded down her back, nearly weightless. *Did he damage my wings?* she thought.

Impossible, Clarin replied. *I would have to be terribly incapacitated for such a thing to occur.* Clarin leaned into the doorway.

The alarm might go, thought Diana.

Yes, prepare yourself, Clarin answered, and she blasted the lock with a burst of firebreath. Nothing sounded. Clarin led Diana inside.

I think I can feel them, Diana realized.

Her thought was barely conscious to herself, but the dragon matriarch replied, *Yes, my children are here. They are hurting.*

The mistcrystal transmitted a kind of ache. Its usual temperature, slightly warmer than Diana's human core, cooled noticeably.

We are led by their pain, lamented the mother dragon, as the two crept around the corner into a giant, high-ceilinged utility room.

Can you tell which way? Diana managed to transmit, her mind pulled from the question by the glinting array of danger that hung on the walls surrounding them. Here, even things her family had in their garage looked menacing: shovels, spades, and hoes took on a threatening presence among the scythes, knives, machetes, crossbows, and guns. A rattling rang out from beyond the door opposite them.

Clarin flew to the top of a large metal cabinet, ordering Diana, *Hide behind it.* There was not enough room for Diana to maneuver into flight. Clarin watched the door, ready to repel anything that entered. Diana felt and heard the refrain in Clarin's mind: *minimum harm, maximum stewardship.* The rattling resumed, but it did not come from the door. A metal box housing some sort of power source had hummed to life.

Who knows what that powers, Diana thought, *probably his own, private shock-therapy room.*

I fear you are not far off, thought Clarin.

What? Diana cried.

I feel them hurting.

Diana asked again, *Where are they?*

I feel only a tangle of their energies. Four of them are very close. She flew down from the cabinet, settling next to Diana. *I feel Ayan, his heartfire muted and warped in confusion, farther away in this terrible place.*

Diana's phone buzzed. *It's Nicki.* She read the text, Clarin following in her mind: *Illsworth and men driving out of town. Don't know if he's headed there yet. Sheriff following. More soon.* The same information came through from Jake's dad a second later.

The sound of voices from beyond the door to the harrowing utility area motivated Clarin to lead the way out of the room. As Diana's eyes adjusted—Clarin's did so instantly—details began to be revealed in the dimness. *I'd rather be in the dark,* Diana thought, realizing they were being regarded by half a dozen game trophies, this time small animals. A raccoon that Diana was *sure* was not full-grown glared at them from a table where it stood in eternal mid-step. There was a hawk and several owls; Diana noted the markings, suspecting they were protected or endangered. *A rabbit,* thought Diana. It wasn't even a big, shaggy jack rabbit, not that she would have found that comforting. It was small, soft, sweet. Its pink eyes stared innocently, seeming to follow them as if to wish them a better fate.

Diana! Clarin warned, breaking the girl's thoughts from the forsaken menagerie. *Follow!* Some of the men sounded close, like they were entering from outside into the utility-room-turned-arsenal.

Clarin took off, Diana in her draft; both achieved a low, steady glide through the large room and then into a wide, stone hallway. Clarin's magic pulled at Diana's elementor with extra insistence, keeping her close. They came to a graceful stop just before an imposing, wooden door made of wide planks, rounded at the top to form an arch and attached with giant, black hinges. Diana had seen many such constructions while peering over at Jake and Nicki's medieval RPG. *Where does he find this stuff?* she thought, feeling she was in one of these video games, wishing the possibility of multiple "lives" came with this scenario.

They have no idea we are here, Clarin assured her. Diana picked up the thought, feeling better.

Open it? Diana thought, her hand on the knob.

Slowly, Clarin replied.

Diana turned the knob. She pushed the heavy door as a creaking hinge announced them in what seemed like a trumpet blast. They entered the empty room, and Diana closed the door carefully, the grating metal of the hinge betraying them the whole time. She sighed in relief.

They are here, Clarin thought. She flew across the room in one swoop, landing next to another door, this one also heavy wood. A bright line of light appeared like a strip of neon under the door. Diana ran to join Clarin. More texts buzzed into her phone: *Illsworth on the move. He's nine miles away, 20 minutes minimum in traffic.*

Clarin heard the content of the text as it ran through Diana's mind, but did not respond. She seemed frozen. Diana's mistcrystal whirred discordantly between heat and coolness, beating and humming. She felt a jumble of unintelligible impressions in her mind, as if many languages were being spoken at once, and she understood none of them.

My children. Clarin swayed. A strange, intense light appeared from underneath a large, oaken door. A closet? A bathroom? *My children.* Clarin steadied herself. *That light is worrisome.* She inched nearer to the door.

Diana questioned her, *Is it like sunlight? It's so bright.*

Yes, the wavelengths are the same, but as if somehow altered or intensified.

Will it hurt you if it's just for a minute?

I may be able to function, but we cannot risk my powers wavering right now.

Clarin stood back and crouched before the slip of light underlining the door. *The firefog,* she thought to Diana, then inhaled hugely and began to effuse the haze of warm, pure, mineral "smoke."

The blazing rays decreased as if on a dimmer switch. Diana opened the door and ran in, Clarin behind her. *Find the power source to the light,* Clarin instructed. Diana heard another inhalation and more firefog filled the room.

I've got it! Diana cried out in her mind, almost letting it escape from her lips. With groping hands, she followed a thick cord from the tall array of panels emitting the burning yellow-white light. She reached the outlet, a square, heavy-duty port, and tugged on the oversized plug. She pulled again with all her might, falling backward as the connector dislodged. The menacing lights went out. And the sirens in the house went on.

Chapter Seventeen

The Found Five

Diana's hands flew to her ears. She swayed, the blaring noise and firefog causing a wave of sickening disorientation. She spun around, her eyes trying to sift through the dim, murky air for Clarin. *Here!* Clarin called to her. Her voice cut through the chaos. Diana stumbled toward Clarin. *Here they are*, said the mother dragon, her unwavering tone a denial of the pandemonium.

In the dissipating firefog, there they were: Merac, Tethys, Tynan, and Gryn, pale versions of themselves, eyes wilting, each looking out from a tiny cage made of cold, gray metal. Diana felt she could cut herself just by looking at the sharp edges. The bottoms of their prisons were lined with shed scales. Those of the ghost dragon were triple the volume of the others. The sun and sea's sloughed scales were so pale, they were barely distinguishable from the cast-offs of the ghost. The scales of the terra appeared as their normal, earthen color, but without their sheen and in far less numbers than those of the other dragons.

Diana approached Tynan, the ghost. *Oh, oh...*Diana could not manage to form words at the devastating sight of him. He was so transparent all his bones showed through a blanched, yellowy hide reminiscent of old onion skins. He lay in an arc, not moving, his heartfire completely invisible in the thinning firefog.

Diana moved between the cages of Merac, the sun, and Tethys, the sea. As she looked from one to the other, she felt Clarin pulling on her thoughts, but she could not tear her sinking heart from the dragons' wretchedness.

Merac lay with his head falling on his fore-talons, eyes closed, the heartfire that should be a blazing crimson showing only faintly: a wilted red rose petal at the bottom of a shallow pond. Tethys lay on her side, her head cast back. What normally appeared as a gleaming, aqua quartz frill around her face now blended into the drained pallor of her aqua scales. Her dull green-blue heartfire throbbed within her like an internal bruise.

Only the terra, Gryn, gave off a moderate cast of her innate coloring and luster. She was the first to respond to the presence of their long-lost mother and this adopted dragonkin girl. Gryn stood on shaky legs and pecked her snout through the caging. Clarin, having gone directly to the young terra's cage, reached for her daughter and connected with her in the *kelling kiss*. At this, Diana's mistcrystal whirred to a new level of life and energy. She looked to Clarin, then back to the tortured dragons, though she didn't need to see the heartfires of the other three captives enliven— she felt it. Merac, Tethys, and Tynan opened their eyes, becoming aware of their liberators.

Doors slammed in another part of the house. Illsworth's thugs would surely make a beeline for the hostage dragons. Diana gripped the latch on the first cage, wherefrom Merac watched her with longing, his rosy face sad and hopeful. The latch did not budge. *I think it's electronic or something*, she thought. Clarin broke from her daughter to stand to the side, then blasted fire on the mechanism. The door popped open. Diana pulled the fragile sun son from the terrible dwelling as Clarin broke the locks on the other cages. All four were free.

She gathered her suffering children to her, pulling them securely within her circled wings. *There isn't time for a proper firesaving for each of you.* She inhaled quickly and exhaled through her burning terra scales and immediately some of the color returned to the four children. The firefog had completely faded now, and Diana beheld the scene, the steadfast stance of the shining mother surrounding the four kidnapped dragons, an emotional Mt. Everest too monumental to take in even as the glory appeared before her.

Footsteps and shouting approached. Gryn broke from her mother's grasp and pointed the way with her body. Diana followed first, supporting the terra daughter when she faltered on her withered limbs. Merac, Tethys, and Tynan hobbled in front of their mother. Diana looked back to see a mother duck nosing her babies forward as they stumbled and fell; but these offspring, though gaunt with deprivation, approached their mother's stature.

Diana ran forward and opened the door toward which Gryn led them. She peeked through. The voices seemed farther away on this side. Gryn walked to the doorway and waited, her footing coming back by degrees, her scales now at half-brilliance. Diana scooped up Tethys and Merac, who could not yet propel themselves, and Clarin, standing on her hind legs and stroking her wings slowly for balance, reached for Tynan with her forelimbs and lifted him like a newborn baby.

Can you fly, my daughter? Clarin thought, including Diana in the telepathy. Gryn nodded to her mother, surely sending her thoughts as well, but Diana could not hear the telepathy of the daughter dragon. Clarin shared her next reply, *Very well, Gryn, but fly with care.* Clarin leaned into Diana, protectively shifting her ghost son and peering down the dim hallway. After adjusting her awkward but iron hold on the sun and sea, Diana shook out her own wings and the elementor re-formed itself along her back.

Follow me, Clarin said, and three sets of terra wings quivered at the ready.

~

"That's not the regular alarm!" Linda Santos cried, a long, sharp weed-pulling tool in her hand, which she held out unconsciously like a spear. Every neighbor in the valley recognized all-too-well Illsworth's "normal," thunderous house alarm. Dr. Kim and Nicki aimed their binoculars at the house, both sweeping to and fro, seeking the source of the upsetting sound. It seemed to come from all around. Jake was on the bumper of the car, also peering through binoculars, passing his vision from the grounds to the roof to the doors, hoping to catch any sign of movement.

"Illsworth is on Rolling Road," Nicki said, reading a text from Sheriff Gonzales.

"Tell my dad he needs to get out here."

"He's on his way," Nicki replied.

"There!" Linda Santos pointed toward the center of the house. The attack birds had been released. A fluttering ceiling of black obscured the blue sky, as the venue of vultures—dozens of them—flew out in a mass before breaking off in all directions.

"They're fanning out," Dr. Kim said, as she pulled Jake off the bumper and motioned for all of them to get behind the car.

The vultures began to circle the grounds, flying in groups of five or six to the edges of the fence, some just beyond it, and others covering the extensive surfaces of the sprawling rooftops. One posse disappeared into the far edge of the avocado grove.

"Some of them are coming this way," Mrs. Santos said, looking a dozen yards west, toward the side of the mansion. She crouched behind the Subaru, her ad-hoc spear still poised for damage.

"What if...what if they *all* come this way?" Nicki said, quietly at first. The others turned to her, understanding dawning on their faces. They grabbed their domestic weaponry and moved, as if choreographed, out from behind the car. Jake started for the fence, impatient to lure the birds in his direction.

"Hold on," Nicki hissed. Switching to a backward trot, Jake spun to face her but maintained his direction. She read from her phone. Jake's dad was almost there. He had taken a dirt road to the north of the property and would come out behind them on the other side of the tiny creek any minute.

"We're fine then; let's go," Jake called back while turning once again toward his objective.

"The more we draw to us, the fewer get to Diana and Clarin," Nicki shouted as she joined Jake. Dr. Kim and Linda formed the follow-up, flanking the youths and brandishing the implements of defense.

"Here, birds!" Nicki shouted, poking the air with a sharp spade on a handle as tall as she was.

"Come on!" Jake wielded his hoe like a medieval flag, daring the vultures to knock the colors from his brave grip.

A group of the scraggy birds veered in the air and aimed for the interlopers, a shifty black "V" picking up speed and definition, until each of the defenders could clearly make out the threatening beaks and talons. The band of four backed up in unison, seeking to use the lowest branches of the avocado trees to shrink the aerial battleground.

The tactic worked too well, and the vultures began to break off, as if the danger had been neutralized, so the human opponents re-emerged from their cover and renewed their antagonistic dances. This time, the vultures broke into two levels, and the low-flyers pierced the safety zone above the car, slamming themselves into the waving instruments that Jake, Nicki, and the two women, now taking harbor behind the hatchback, stabbed into the air. Jake and Nicki ran closer to the car and flanked Dr. Kim and Linda Santos.

More vultures appeared, diving at the party from the sides. Mrs. Santos pulled Nicki to her side, raising her weapon high and swishing it over their heads, establishing a protective rhythm with Dr. Kim, as Jake jabbed to the side. "Oh," Jake cried out, a wincing look of regret twisting his features as the hoe landed on the birds' ultimately very slight bodies.

Several vultures hit them from a concerted attack path just off center, flying inches above the hood of the car and drawing all their defenses at once. At that moment, two more careened from the side into Linda Santos's unprotected head and shoulder. As she ducked and covered her head, trying to pull Nicki down to relative safety, two more birds appeared behind those. Even more escaped from the house and grounds, a stream of ebony hostility to reinforce the onslaught.

Jake jumped out from his side of the shelter and swung his hoe in a 360-degree arc, his shouts practically a match for the screeching of the marauders.

"Get back here," Mrs. Santos yelled, but the proximity of the attackers prevented any action by her or the other two whom Jake now championed.

Jack shouted back, "We have to keep them occupied!" Everyone flinched as with each blow he struck bird after bird. He sent them reeling into the trees—tangles of crooked feathers thrashing among the leaves—or knocked them into spirals of flight before they landed in heaps of disarray on the dusty ground.

The shrieks of the injured birds gained the attention of more birds, and before any of the other three could stop it, a dozen greasy, sharp-beaked, savages pummeled Jake, his swinging wood and metal no match for their numbers. He sank to his knees, the darkening mass descending upon him, tearing and scratching at him relentlessly. One or more of the assailants managed to accidentally knock the handle from Jake's grasp, and still, he would have gone at the birds with only his hands, were he able to inflict punishment and protect his eyes at the same time. Nicki and Mrs. Santos ran nearer to his aid, the birds pecking at their moving bodies anywhere they could strike. Dr. Kim hung back and aimed the tranquilizer gun, but she was unable to find a remotely clear shot amidst the wild raiders surrounding Jake.

What seemed like dozens more birds made their way to join the fray. Nicki and Mrs. Santos fended off more attackers, thrusting at them ineffectively, since their need to guard their eyes undermined their aim. They were now at risk of becoming as inundated by the vicious venue of vultures as Jake, who curled up into a ball as his would-be rescuers crawled toward him, their defenses at the point of extinction, their arms waving at the predatory shroud of aggression. Dr. Kim once again advanced with the tranquilizer gun.

A shot rang out. A few birds on the periphery flew off, but the central mass remained dedicated to its strike. Another shot tore through the animal din, several feet above the bedraggled human party. The second shot quieted all but the most ferocious of the carrion creatures. Then, with a sickening thud, a body fell from the air, brushing against Nicki and landing on her feet. She jumped back with a small shriek and stared at the bleeding bird. The sheriff, holstering his gun in favor of his nightstick, ran to his son, waving the baton in fury and slamming it into the remaining half-dozen vultures until most of them broke off. Dr. Kim and Linda rushed up and arched themselves over Jake, Nicki running to their side to join Sheriff Gonzales in fending off the last few birds.

~

In the house, Gryn flew from the small, smoky chamber into the enormous hallway, followed by Diana at a run, her dragon cargo too unwieldy for her to take to flight. Clarin rose gracefully into the cramped airspace, her ghost son in her arms, her slightly retracted wings beating quickly. Behind them, men's angry shouts echoed through the now-empty light chamber. Heavy footsteps followed, closing in.

Gryn flew in an erratic pattern at first, grazing the stone walls and upsetting a stand topped with a sleek, spotted startling turned taxidermic. Her coordination was that of a child's when first learning to ride a bike, but her direction was sure. She ducked through a doorway toward a brightly lit area. Diana, via a low, shaky flight, tailed her, with Clarin following deftly, her senses sharp. At a turn in the hall up ahead, the light spilled from an oversized doorway. The party of fliers entered an expansive foyer outside a huge, somewhat grimy industrial kitchen. Most of the light was coming from an oversized skylight dominating half the ceiling.

The vulture release! Diana thought, relief at the possibility of escape rounding out her words. Gryn aimed for the opening, but as she approached the apex, the doors started to slide shut. Gryn darted back into the room, unwilling to separate herself from the others.

"Get them!" one of Illsworth's men shouted, brandishing a spear-headed staff, while the other aimed a dart rifle at Clarin. A thin, pale, snide-looking man spoke into a radio on his sleeve, "In the vulture den. Get in here."

Diana, a fledgling flyer with an awkward bundle, could not hover well. She wobbled and shifted, her head just inches from the high ceiling. She took one deep breath and sent a commanding surge of energy to her elementor and felt herself regain composure.

The control, she and Clarin both thought at once. Gryn was already flying toward a black unit on the wall that looked like a garage door opener. The young terra's uncertainty diminished with each stroke of wing. She flew at the guards, dodging and weaving in the air, drawing one guard to wave his weapon and miss. The other took aim at Clarin, but Diana positioned herself in front of the dragon, and the man hesitated, his face perplexed as he shouted, "How's the kid doing this? And what the heck do I do with her?"

While he hesitated, Gryn got around the other stumbling thug, this one shouting to his partner, "Get the skinny one! It's going to open the doors!" With that, Gryn landed on the button and the doors began their slide. The pencil-nosed guard near her swung his staff and struck her in the side, throwing her to the tile amidst the filthy vulture leavings and bits of drying feeder flesh. Gryn lay on the foul floor, breath heaving, but otherwise motionless. The skylight doors opened.

Go, thought Clarin to Diana, but Diana could not leave them. *Get Merac and Tethys to safety.*

I can't leave you. Give me Tynan, Diana insisted back with her mind, staying between Clarin and the dart-gunner.

"I'll have to shoot you, kid," the man yelled, as the escape in the ceiling opened far enough to permit Diana's exit. On the floor, the skinny goon reached for Gryn, who was just shaking herself to awareness. The gunner took aim at Diana. *Go!* Clarin insisted again.

From below them rose hair-raising, snarling growls. Shark, her jaw pulled back to reveal gleaming, dripping fangs, the fur on her back bristling, threw herself between Gryn and the advancing thug. Shark and Alcatraz rounded on the stocky gunman, their jowls slack and oozing drool as they bared their huge teeth and threatened to jump on him. He commanded the dogs—"Down!"—to no effect, and the huge animals easily pushed him to the floor, biting and pulling his shirt and wrangling until the guard lost his grip on the rifle. From his position beneath the enraged beasts, the man flailed among the droppings and filth in a fruitless effort to try to re-clutch the tranquilizer gun.

Gryn shot up to her mother and Diana, and the three flew toward the the rendezvous point. Within moments, a barrage of vultures barrelled toward them. They flew high above the electrical barrier, Diana grappling with the two bony dragons, who had regained enough awareness to wriggle in her arms as they made the uncomfortable vertical ascent and descent. Gryn flew close to this new dragon-human, watching for a chance to intercede should one of her siblings start to slip.

Diana saw her mother's car, right where they had planned. She held tight to Merac and Tethys, not daring to adjust her grasp, though both of the frail creatures now unwittingly scratched at her arms. Diana landed and her mother ran to her, reaching out to receive a dragon, to which Diana responded by placing the sun, Merac, into Linda Santos's arms. "So pale," Mrs. Santos murmured, as she hurried toward the car. Dr. Kim took Tethys and joined Linda in settling them in the vehicle.

Nicki ran to Clarin, who had lain Tynan down on a patch of grass, where she regarded her tortured child. Tynan labored to breathe, his skin pulling in over his bones with each inhalation, accentuating his emaciation. Yellowed scales, like battered, weathered sequins, fell from him, sprinkling the grass like forgotten confetti. Clarin bent her head to her son. Diana heard the anguished mother's thoughts, *His breath is too cool. He's far more depleted than the others.* Clarin covered her son like a blanket and exuded as much firesaving as time would allow. The ghost's frail frame looked even more damaged with his increased heartfire. But Diana could at least feel Clarin breathing easier, for now.

"Don't worry," Nicki said, as she stood by in witness. But tears began to flow as she digested Tynan's wasted condition, his lightless eyes. Clarin let Nicki lift the precious dragon child and carry him to the others. Gryn approached her mother, whose shape and markings were echoed in her own form. She lay by her side for just a moment, their heartfires matching tempo. Nearing Jake, Diana turned to glance back at the terras, the harmony of her mistcrystal assuring her that these restored connections in the dragon family had already strengthened them all.

Then Diana saw Jake. He lay on the grass and dirt, his father's jacket beneath him, a blanket from her mom's car folded under his head. His eyes were closed. Scratches and cuts appeared like broken pick-up sticks across his cheeks and arms. His blue t-shirt was torn from the side, obliterating part of the bluejay mascot on his school baseball jersey. The gaping shirt revealed a bloody, dusty scratch so long it disappeared around his back.

Diana fell to Jake's side. His father was looking him over, checking for breaks or excessive bleeding, saying to him, "We have to get you—everyone—out of here, now."

Jake sighed loudly, "Well, what are you waiting for?" He tried to laugh, wincing and grabbing his side, then exclaimed, "Ouch!" as he touched his bloody cut with his salty hand.

Diana started to laugh, to which Jake opened one eye and peered at her suspiciously, but he smiled weakly. Diana said, "Sorry. I'm just glad you're OK enough to be so lame."

Diana looked at the heap of lifeless feathers on the ground, shocked. Even with the battles, she never wished the poor things real harm. *Illsworth: everything he touched just had to suffer*. Dr. Kim appeared next to them, another of Linda's blankets in hand. She and the sheriff helped Jake up, wrapped him in the scratchy wool, and walked him past the Santos' car and through the thin trees. His father took over, half carrying him over the trickle of summer stream to the black and white sheriff's car beyond. "I'll be back in one minute," his father said while Jake delicately pulled the seatbelt over his aching body, adjusting it to avoid the gash on his side.

Sheriff Gonzales ran back to the others. He arrived to see Diana and Dr. Kim placing a cloth over the dead vulture, then gently rolling it into the shroud. "Here, let me," he called. "I'll put it in my trunk."

Diana and Dr. Kim acquiesced, while Diana heard Clarin's reminder: *We can learn much from this tragic creature.* Dr. Kim opened her mouth to speak, but the sheriff was already offering what she was about to request.

"I'll take it straight to your place. I understand." As the sheriff gathered the bundle, he said, "Illsworth was just a few minutes behind me." He turned toward Linda. "Can you follow me over the short cut? The road's pretty rough but mostly dried out now."

"Of course," answered Linda. "We don't want to pass Illsworth on the way home."

Clarin spoke to Diana, who relayed aloud, "Clarin was going to go back for Ryan—" Diana's voice broke as a fraction of the mother dragon's feelings coursed through the mistcrystal and broke her heart, "But she knows she can't." They all looked over at Clarin and the rescued dragons, the mother minus one child. Clarin stood like a guardian over the four, her eyes shining, but sad.

"I'll ride with Jake," Nicki offered. Diana looked puzzled and was about to question her. "I'll get the vulture into the lab space. That way if anything—" she gulped, "—should delay you guys, Sheriff G. can just go take care of Jake."

"Thanks, Nicki." Diana might have run over and hugged her quiet friend, but Nicki was already running after Jake's dad. Diana turned and got in the car, telling Dr. Kim and her mom what was happening.

"That's our Nicki," both women said at once, and they all got to smile for a moment.

"Text her to lock up, even with the deputy outside," Dr. Kim added. Linda started the car and gingerly backed it out, making a three-point turn that gave them all a last look at the terrible house. Mrs. Santos sped along the few yards where they were visible from Illsworth's, then turned east and gunned it on the dry road through the oaks. As they receded from the area, Diana thought she heard the alarms stop, though she wasn't sure if they had simply gone beyond its range. The air got quiet. Diana heard some of Clarin's soothings to her children. She looked behind to see three terrorized dragons sleeping in a pile: skinny, hairless, pastel kittens, whose pallid heartfires, together, added up to the luminosity of just one of their healthy dragonling siblings. Their terra sister, awake, rested against them and watched their mother.

Diana looked over the seat, part of her brain still in disbelief that they had found and freed these dragon children. She heard Clarin's lamentation and declaration, spoken in a voice of stone covered in softness, *Ayan, my child. Hold on. I feel you. We are coming back for you.*

Chapter Eighteen

Discoveries and Dragondregs

In deep darkness, Shay sheltered his four returned dragon children. Their resuscitation from the unceasing light exposure—and therefore darkness deprivation—became his heartfire's calling. Scraping healthy scales from his own wing into a fire circle in front of him, he melted them, calling his children close to inhale the hallowed blue fumes. They breathed out onto the scorching scales, releasing the toxins from their centers, then drew in the mixed exhalations of their own and one-another's damaged cores, along with their father's strong medicinal smoke. Through this mineral synthesis, their own harmful accumulations were replaced by the magically infused cells of their father's firebreath.

Shay cooled his children's bodies with breaths of warm steam that beaded up and dripped from their fatigued frames. This expedited a rest period between mineral exchanges that would have otherwise taken many hours of darkness to achieve. Soon, the terra would be one hundred percent restored, and a firesavings from Clarin would complete the healing for the other three.

~

Upstairs, Diana, Nicki, and Dr. Kim stood over a cold, bare metal table in the veterinary lab space—formerly a large mudroom—at the back of Dr. Kim's house. Clarin perched on the end of the table, regarding the creature with compassion. The vulture, whom a latex-gloved Dr. Kim had rolled out of the blanket, stared at them with glassy eyes. Stiffness was beginning to set in. Its red splotches of flesh now appeared gray and clammy. Diana shivered. Dr. Kim looked closely at the bird. "I'm not sure what we can learn by autopsy when there is magic involved. This is certainly new territory."

Nicki pointed to the strange device hanging around its neck. "Well, we should probably start there, anyway."

Diana steeled herself and touched the little black box, the one they had seen on all the vultures, the one bearing the ouroboros.

Dr. Kim turned to a drawer behind her and reached for masks and goggles. "Here," she said. "I don't know about magic, but I know the message from Jeff said '*beware.*'" She finished quietly, aware of the feebleness of the caution, given the circumstances.

The girls put on the plastic eye shields and masks without argument. Dr. Kim took a pair of clippers from the drawer and snipped the cord holding the device. It fell onto the table with a tinny clang. Diana reached for it, picked it up, and shook it.

"There's something inside," Diana said, holding the slim vessel to her ear and shaking again. "It's super light."

"Here, let me," Dr. Kim insisted, as if determined to shelter these twelve-year-old heroes from *something* if she could. She felt for any give on the box, finally applying pressure to the back in a way that caused the front to pop open. Pale, olive-colored dust filled the room.

Clarin stiffened. She screeched once and fell forward. Her slight frame landed on the dead vulture and half rolled, half slid off the feathered corpse. Nicki moved quickly to catch the mother dragon in an awkward hold, preventing the unconscious dragon from falling off the table.

Diana screamed, grabbed at her throat, and seemed to faint. She slid sideways toward the cold tile floor. Dr. Kim thrust an arm under one of Diana's just in time to pull her back and keep her from hitting her head on the edge of the steel table.

Diana's mind flailed at the edge of consciousness but could still see and hear. "Get them out of here," Dr. Kim cried, as Diana tried to get her feet to function beneath her. Nicki had Clarin in a cradle hold and was running to the living room. Dr. Kim supported Diana down the hallway to the couch, then ran back toward the lab space and surveyed the scene from as far across the hallway as possible. Dr. Kim and Nicki both seemed fine. Diana appeared behind her and touched her on the shoulder, giving her a little shock.

"You're all right?" Dr. Kim exclaimed, sighing with relief as she hugged Diana briefly.

"I feel perfectly normal, but whatever happened to Clarin went right through me for a second," Diana said.

Dr. Kim leaned in, extending her arm as far as possible to catch the door, and closed it on the disturbing little morgue. She took an old towel from behind her in the linen closet, tucked it into the space under the door, and the two dashed back to check on Clarin, who, they were surprised and happy to see, now appeared perfectly fine.

"*Dragondregs*," Diana said out loud, repeating the word Clarin put in her mind.

"Dragondregs?" Dr. Kim and Nicki turned the word over together.

"The shed scales of the kidnapped dragons, collected, powdered, and imbued with some kind of ancient magic," Diana continued to tell the other two as Clarin told her, "the scales of abused dragons, light-tormented, darkness-deprived." They stared at her as she finished, "Stolen, taboo magic. Stuff Clarin says she doesn't even really understand."

"So that makes the shiftcrystal and now this," Nicki said, disgusted, tossing her head in the general direction of Illsworth's manor.

"And heaven knows what else..." Dr. Kim said.

Diana knelt in front of Clarin. She looked in her eyes. She put her hand to her mistcrystal and knew what she would hear:

The QuinKell.

The QuinKell. And she said aloud, "The Quinkell."

Pounding on the front door roused the four of them. "Coming," said Dr. Kim, looking out the window before opening, even though the deputy guarded the house. "Come in!"

Linda Santos had ahold of Brody's shirt. She let go and he ran in. "Sorry, he's just so worked up," she apologized.

Brody stopped to sit in front of Clarin and Diana, looking widely into the face of the golden dragon, then to his sister. "What's wrong?" he asked.

Brody said it so sweetly Diana bit back a tear, then sighed, smiled at her brother, and said, "Nothing." She glanced at Clarin, then stood and held out her hand. "Come on," she said to her brother while tossing her head at Nicki to join them, "there are four more dragons home." She started to lead Brody out of the living room, then turned back to look at Clarin.

"I'll bring her down when she's ready. And I think it's a good idea if I keep an eye on her for a bit," said Dr. Kim. Diana smiled gratefully and continued out with her brother.

Jake was coming in the kitchen door when Diana entered with Brody. His father, key in hand, winked at the kids and closed the door again, returning to coordinating with the deputy and preparing to leave for his other, non-dragon-related duties.

Jake was dotted with bandages, yellowish splotches of antiseptic bleeding out over his dark skin from underneath the first-aid patches. Other places, the jaundiced protectant painted swaths across the thin cuts all over his arms. His face was nearly untouched. The girls stared. "I know, I look like a reverse-bruised banana," Jake said, flashing a smile at his own wit.

"You're all right?" Nicki said, while Diana peered down toward his side, as if she would be supplied with x-ray vision to examine the huge scrape there. Jake touched his flank, affected a minor, semi-sincere wince, then patted it and declared, "No biggie. No stitches." The girls smiled as Brody tugged at Diana, and they all descended into the basement dragon den.

Brody make a beeline for the darkened corner where the rescued dragons slept, dew-covered, around their father. Diana made the *shhh* signal and the four children simply stood looking at the four injured dragons. "Aww," Brody whispered, "they look like Clarin and Shay. I didn't think they'd be so big."

"They're only about three years old," Nicki said.

Brody, remembering to whisper, said, "I'm a lot older than them."

"But they're full grown," his sister replied.

Brody made a move closer, and Diana reached for him. "Don't worry, I'm not going to touch," he said. Shay shifted his eyes to meet Diana's across the cool dimness and nodded.

"It's OK, it would actually be good for them," she told her brother, to more nods from the father dragon. "Just be very, very gentle." Diana and her friends all stepped forward and reached for the dragon closest to them, like they'd each been personally assigned to one. Diana stroked Tynan with one finger along his white chest, and Brody copied the gentle petting on Merac's dark red wing. Jake held out his hand and lightly petted Tethys, and Nicki stroked little Gryn, who was not only awake, but also looked like a pet cat as she arched her spine for more.

Shay breathed a visible sigh and nodded again to Diana. She put her hand over Brody's and pulled gently to direct him over to the nest of healthy hatchlings. Jake and Nicki followed. The seas, suns, ghost and terra all tumbled together, one spreading its wings and flapping frenetically in a kind of "leap-dragon" over the next. Brody stuck his hand out so a little sea landed on it, and the other dragons accepted the seven-year-old's hand as part of their chain of obstacles. He giggled as each dragon baby hopped and hobbled across his hand, until a sun dug its growing talons in a little too deeply. "Hey!" Brody exclaimed, but laughed as he pulled his hand back and rubbed the tiny scratch.

The little terra perched near her siblings' riotous game and watched as two suns collided above the ghost and a sea. At this, she stretched her amber wings and sailed—her strokes only slightly choppy—a few inches over the whole pile. A sea jumped up and nipped at her back feet as she floated down, causing her to tumble to a landing. Brody laughed, pointing to the mischievous sea. The sea was now irritating the terra with more nips and pecks, looking for a reaction. "That one's my favorite!" Brody cried.

"Look at this one!" Jake said in a convincing imitation of little Brody's enthusiasm. He pointed to a sun who was aiming its firebreath at a pink scale and attempting to warm it slowly by increasing the intensity of its tiny fire stream.

Nicki looked over. "The sun's adaptation! Varying temperatures of firebreath!"

Jake looked at her, admiringly at first, then snapped his head back and to the side, a lightbulb going on, and said, "Oh, yeah! The *fireflow.*" Jake looked at Nicki with satisfaction. "I wonder if we'll get to see the little seas make steam?"

"*That's* called the *firemist*," Nicki said, returning Jake's smug look but then smiling broadly.

"Whatcha doing?" Jake called over, his attention diverted to where Brody had broken away from the little pack and now bent his body so his face was level with the ledge, his chin almost resting on the dusty cement.

Brody picked something up. Nicki zipped to his side. "What's this?" the little boy asked, holding up and turning over a dark gray, spherical object that looked rough like tree bark but had a chalky exterior. "It feels like charcoal for our grill," he said, bringing it close to his face. "Ew, smells like it, too—but, yech, too stinky." He held it away and turned to hold it up in the light from the window. Tiny flecks of red and orange appeared in the dark briquette.

Jake had come over. He muffled a laugh. "What?" Brody asked. Nicki smiled at him, but when he tried to give her his new find, she put her hands behind her back and shook her head, also smiling.

"You can actually crush it up," Jake said, a twinkle in his eye. Brody, unaccustomed to being given such permission, regarded his sister's friend with suspicion. But it was too tempting. He pressed his hands together and crushed the lump. It crumbled instantly into fine dust like powdered sugar and released a sweet, smoky scent. "Now it smells kinda good," he said, bringing his hands nearer to his face. "Ugh..." he grimaced, "...kinda." Residual warmth from the pellet's core spread through his hands. "Wow!" he cried. "It's warm, like the dragons."

Jake, laughing aloud now, could contain himself no longer. "That's because it's—"

Nicki took over, starting to giggle herself, "That's because it's *from* the dragons." Brody stared at her, cocking his head to the side like his dog listening for a command. "It's how they...eliminate," she continued. "Do you know what an owl pellet is?"

Brody jerked his head back over his shoulders and nearly shouted, "We see them on the field at school! They have rat bones, and sometimes cat bones, in them!" His eyes bulged in what the older children mistook for alarm. He squinted at the residue his hands. "Too bad worms don't have bones..." he said, disappointed, and brushed his hands on his pants, walking back toward the hatchlings and muttering, "...dragon pellets: so cool."

Clarin appeared at the top of the stairs, apparently fully recovered from the dragondregs episode. Jake ran over as soon as he saw the light. He hopped to the top step and presented his back to the beautiful dragon, which they had all agreed was preferred to dragons navigating narrow, wooden stairs. Clarin climbed on, and then a few seconds later, as Jake bent himself into a human drawbridge, climbed off onto the nest area.

Diana came over. "Clarin says she needs me to relieve Shay at watching over the recovering ones," she said to Jake, Nicki looking over to stay in the loop, though she found it difficult to pull her attention from a little sun's white-hot fireflow practice.

Diana walked to the back of the den and surveyed the healing dragons. The sun and sea had regained about half their normal coloring, and the terra glowed at a depth beginning to resemble her mother's. The ghost lay close to his father. The cast of Shay's blue-green gleam looked like waves washing down the sleeping dragon's back and dissolving into frothy surf over the pearl-colored legs and feet. Diana reached for Shay's snout and stroked him; he looked so steady and powerful in all his quiet. He broke her gaze and flapped down off of the ledge, skipped off the floor like a stone on water to settle next to his mate.

Clarin included Diana in her thoughts to Shay: *The QuinKell, the children.* Diana felt a little like an eavesdropper. *Be still. I want you to hear,* Clarin said, replying to the thoughts Diana had not even fully formed to herself. Diana quieted, watching the four dragons sleep. She leaned on the ledge, her face close to the terra, who opened her eyes and gazed into Diana's. They stayed like that, Diana a welcome sister among these young adults of the dragonkin.

One of each must make the sacrifice, Diana heard. Gryn's eyes widened. She remained still. Silence. Shay must have been responding. Gryn raised her head a fraction of an inch, looking toward her parents. Diana heard Clarin's voice, a gentle rejoinder to the terra daughter, *Sleep, my child. This does not concern you.* Diana reached for Gryn's front talons and gently patted her, trying for a motion that would emulate Clarin's tone. Clarin continued, *My terra child should not be able to hear my sheltered thoughts*. Clarin exchanged a long look with her mate, then continued, *Shay supposes it may be due to the dragondregs effects; and   I wonder at the power of the unprecedented presence of my mistcrystal among us.*

Rest, Clarin again implored her curious daughter. Gryn placed her head on Diana's hand as it lay over the young dragon's feet and closed her eyes. No one believed she was resting.

"Nicki, Jake!" Diana whisper-shouted. They looked over. "Clarin wants your help. She and Shay need to get outside." Her two friends looked puzzled. Diana continued, "They need to fly."

"I want to help!" Brody chirped.

"Um, OK," Jake said, looking to Nicki with a shrug.

"Will you open the doors for us?" Nicki asked.

"Yep!" The ginger-headed seven-year-old practically tripped up the stairs and waited, his hand on the doorknob before either dragon was even piggybacked. He held the door to the kitchen open as Nicki and Jake carried the dragon pair up into the room, its cheery hues muted in the gathering twilight. Brody ran to the front door. He jumped to try to see through the curtain. Jake stepped forward with Shay, his surprisingly dignified payload, holding onto the boy's growing shoulders.

"Coast is clear," Jake said, glad to see his dad, who had replaced the earlier deputy. Brody struggled with the deadbolt. Jake reached out to help, but Brody slapped his hand away, eliciting a giggle from Nicki, who otherwise bore her dragon passenger with reverence.

Brody exclaimed, "I got it!" as he slowly opened and then held the door with an air that suggested he might salute at any moment. Sheriff Gonzales ran over, wearing a querying expression that bordered on worried. Jake and Nicki sat on the narrow steps, one next to the other, to allow the dragons to step off at the top. The children stood and moved to the side, Jake waving his dad off with a nod and smile. With that, the blue and sable dragons took flight from the landing.

Facing each other, they soared straight up, as close as their wing strokes would allow. Continuing upward, Clarin broke off slightly to her right and Shay also to his; they angled around one another and passed in the air, near enough to graze wings lightly. They arched back away and flew a small arc, then returned to each other, again almost touching and passing on the left side. Up and up they climbed, weaving together in vertical infinity loops, moving faster and faster until they blurred into one smoky, undulating streak.

"Well, I wanted to see more of them. I guess that's a start," said the sheriff, who, with the other human gawkers, attempted through squinting eyes to track the pair as they disappeared like chameleons into the golden and cobalt sunset sky.

The dragon couple continued their looping ascent, brushing heat and nearly brushing bodies, swinging on an imaginary axis from the other's center, until they achieved the height at which the beacons of their children's consciousnesses no longer reached them. They were alone, together, in mind and heart. They adjusted to fly side-by-side in a horizontal path, wing strokes in perfect tandem, wingtips touching every so often. Shay's blue scales blended with the darkening sky, while Clarin turned to russet as she took on the deep gold of the sun as it slipped from the horizon.

They flew to the top of a boulder outcropping, but rather than land, circled the formation slowly, as each metamorphosed into their adaptations of invisibility. Clarin's glowing gold dissipated into a thin smoke, her shape now a light brown veil of its material form. Shay, revolving around his mate, appeared as a dewy cloud. The two continued circling, now a swirl of smoke and mist, with a faint glow of the heartfire contained in each dragon's chest. Faster and faster they swirled until the center of the spinning cloud was inhabited by a blur of gold and blue heartfire that appeared as a single ring of colored light.

Without words, without telepathy, with only the intangible exchange of the most profound communication between a mated dragon pair, their inner beings exchanged the question to resolve:

Clarin's Intention: *I must sacrifice myself to the QuinKell. As the only other adult terra, Gryn must be given the chance to mature, to eventually lead the dragonkin. We have had two broods. I may produce more eggs, but the depletions to my nature from the portal opening—not to mention the strange, stolen magic perpetrated upon us—may threaten that. Gryn must be given a chance to live fully and to help rebuild the dragonkin.*

Shay's Intention: *I must sacrifice myself. As their father, I must serve our dragonkin by submitting myself to the QuinKell, for there are many seas to replace me in our new family. Thought it grieves us, our brave and precious Gryn will gladly give herself as the terra, allowing you to remain as both mother and mentor. And I will join her and our strong sun, Merac, and dear ghost, Tynan. You will regenerate in every way necessary and continue to lead the dragonkin.*

The dragon pair continued the sky-dance, their considerations and responses swirling. As Shay absorbed Clarin's impressions, his heartfire took on an amber tinge; as Clarin absorbed her mate's, her heartfire took on an aqua halo. The line of their joined, moving hearts continued to glow alternately in each of their individual colors, changing intensities and concentrations as it revolved—Clarin's now shining less brightly as she assimilated her husband's reasoning for his sacrifice; Shay's waning slightly as he contemplated accepting the loss of his mate to the ritual.

As they moved, the balance of their intentions began to meld, each entertaining the possibility of giving way, yet only one needing to do so to resolve the question. The chafing, blending, and communing of their beliefs reached a resolution. Both hearts steadied and accepted. Shay's heartfire dimmed momentarily to a silver fog, invisible within his misty apparition. Then it regained its turquoise brilliance. The two dragons re-materialized, slowing the circling flight as their solid physical forms re-emerged. They landed on the large boulder, nestled into each other, and exchanged the *kelling kiss* of the mated pair, heartfires blazing.

Clarin and Shay returned to the nest and gathered their four healing children to them. Each day, the tormented dragons became stronger, beginning to resemble the healthy three-year-olds they would have been, had they not been lost and abused all that time. Diana and the other humankin visited often, taking care to bring extra rations of earthworms for the now ravenous young dragons.

Other than the constant guard by Max Gonzales and Laura Sullivan—as well as several more officers who knew only that violent threats had been made to Dr. Kim and some rare animals she stewarded—a kind of normal rhythm settled in. Illsworth's men had been seen driving slowly past the house, but they did not overstep the law enforcement boundaries.

When, in the next few weeks, the tupi fruits ripened again, Clarin and Shay insisted the four older dragons have it all. At this, Tynan, Merac, Tethys, and Gryn good-humoredly put up with their newly hatched siblings' attempts to pilfer the fruit, though they allowed only bits to be dragged off by the little bandits. Merac, the most affected by the enlivening effects of the fruit, put on shows of fireflow—restrained for indoors, but still mesmerizing—for the younger siblings. As he blackened the cement floor, the baby suns pushed to get closer, eager to witness the nuances of their big brother's sun magic.

Tynan, though he gave special attention to the new baby ghost, seemed somewhat subdued. Everyone mourned Phaed, but missing a new dragon of this nature hit him differently, especially with the knowledge that their other ghost brother was being forced so far astray. Still, when the little one climbed over his brother's talons and looked up at the grown ghost's face, Tynan bared his teeth and let the firecurrent build, though in the basement lair he was careful to reach a peak no more dangerous than a spark of static electricity. The small ghost mimicked the gesture, if not yet the current.

Tethys surrounded herself with the little seas, creating firemist for them to fly around in: a bobbing, sailing hide-and-seek among their personal clouds. One of the new sea children looked almost exactly like Tethys, and she so much like Shay. Clarin had them line up next to their father several times, while the others, both dragons and humans, looked on. They reminded Diana of Brody's and her school photos, all lined up from various stages in the same life.

Gryn was enraptured by the baby terra. No one had expected another terra in this brood. That Clarin had replaced herself in her first hatching of five was a statistical improbability. Most days—although the terra big sister generally spread herself equally among her siblings—she separated off for awhile with the rare little hatchling. Sitting quietly, they exchanged more than they might have with activity. Diana, also interacting frequently with all of the amazing little dragons, seemed always to end up in a conference of three, her mistcrystal a different, richer gold when she convened with the two terras. Gryn could still hear Clarin—apparently somehow through

Diana—even when the mother dragon did not direct her telepathy at her young but mature terra child. Though this complicated the plans Clarin, Shay, and Diana were compelled to make, it also made for a quickly deepening bond among the terras and Diana.

Though the parents delighted in the presence of each of their children, grateful and fulfilled to have four of them back again, their deepest joy came from watching them interact, seeing them grow stronger and grow from one another as they formed the permanent bonds of the dragonkin.

Bittersweet came the day when Clarin, Shay, and Diana acknowledged that the young adult dragons had healed completely. Now they would be drawn into the plan. Now some of them would be asked to give up almost everything; they would be asked to give up the freedom they had just regained.

Chapter Nineteen

The Summoning of the QuinKell

Diana stood with her mistcrystal dangling in front of her eyes as she held it up by its cord. In her other hand she grasped something unseen. Surrounded by a perfect square of four dragons, one of each nature, she looked from one to the next: Tynan, the ghost; Tethys, the sea; Merac, the sun; and Clarin, their mother, the terra.

Each dragon began to breathe a narrow, powerful stream of fire over Diana, toward a spot several feet above her head. The firebreaths shone a hue corresponding to the dragon's nature, coalescing several feet above Diana to form a bright white fountain of light. The white flames seemed to spin at the top of the ten-foot-high spout and gathered like a blazing sun, but without the dangerous heat. A projection of the flame began to build from the center of the ball of fire, extending and receding from the top like a ghostly solar flare.

The glow of the mistcrystal intensified. Diana held her position, her legs quivering but strong. She longed for the steady beat of reassurance the mistcrystal provided when it rested on her throat. The mistcrystal brightened still more until it matched the white light of the fire-fountain. At this, Tynan broke off and flew north.

Almost a mile from Diana, on the exact trajectory of Tynan's northerly path, a transparent sphere outlined in bright white light emerged from the ground. Like a rigid, perfect bubble, it issued as if already whole. Without disturbing the ground, it grew to a height and depth of at least twenty feet.

Although she was still surrounded by three dragons breathing the unwavering *QuinKelling* fire, a cool wind, seeming to arise from nowhere, blew across Diana alone.

She felt something soft and powdery inside her closed hand. A shiver ran through her. *This is it,* she thought. Her hand shook as she loosened her grip just enough to see the first of the scales she held turning to diamond-esque dust. *Tynan is there.* She held her softly clasped fist out to the side and allowed the wind to carry off the superfine particles. Her heart quickened in a mix of grief and anticipation. Diana closed her hand again tightly, watching the white iridescence disperse in the breeze.

Tynan had touched down. From the base of the Northern Sphere arose an eerie white glow. The dragon stood at attention on the glimmering globe, wings spread, head bowed. The rim of the kelling sphere glimmered against the desert ground, a match for Tynan's brightest scales. The inside of the sphere remained transparent; the coastal desert brush could be viewed through it as if the sphere wasn't there. With an inner call heard by Diana and all of the dragonkin, Tynan's ethereal voice rang out:

> *By the dragonkin ancestry—*
> *By the ancient force of the QuinKell—*
> *I submit to the power of the Northern Sphere.*
> *May all who remain find haven*
> *Within our perpetual guardianship.*

Upon the last word, the metamorphic light reached Tynan and engulfed him, transmuting his flesh into sparkling, white gemstone until he appeared as a dragon-shaped diamond himself. The light snuffed out. Atop the shining desert sphere stood an inanimate Tynan, his protective stance turned inward on the emerging QuinKell, the first to give himself as its Sentinel.

Within a few seconds, the color inside the mistcrystal turned from white to red. Merac ended his fire fountain and flew off to the south. Diana waited, the nerves in her hand twitching, ready to sense the next disintegration.

Merac landed upon the Southern Sphere, which was an equal distance from Diana as the Northern Sphere, and perfectly aligned to the south. *Oh, Merac,* thought Diana, as fluorescent red-orange powder slipped from her hand, taken by the strange wind just as the ghost's scale-dust had been.

Merac's touchdown triggered a burning red glow to appear at the sphere's foundation, in the same manner as the white light beneath Tynan. Merac stood surely upon his post with wings spread and head tilted back. The fiery red light spread up to meet him as he finished the pledge of the QuinKell:

> *...I submit to the power of the Southern Sphere*
> *May all who remain find haven*
> *Within our perpetual guardianship.*

The crimson light rose to engulf Merac, who became the second, the ruby, Sentinel.

Diana's mistcrystal changed to glistening seafoam, and Tethys ceased her firebreathing and flew toward the Eastern Sphere. She landed atop the magical beacon.

The sea scale-dust, borne away on the sudden wind, tinted the air around Diana a soft, shimmery teal. She murmured, "Goodbye, Tethys."

Blue-green light overtook the dragon as she finished her pledge. Once the transfiguration was complete, she stood as the third Sentinel of the QuinKell, petrified as brilliant blue-green quartz, wings folded, head bowed.

Clarin and Diana remained. The terra's fire alone cut the air above Diana. The mistcrystal, now its usual color, pulsed with unprecedented fury. Clarin broke off her firebreath. As soon as the fire stream stopped, the light in the mistcrystal burst into a bright white flare and began to levitate at the end of its cord. Diana let go. The mistcrystal, a tiny star, remained suspended in the air before her eyes.

Clarin flew. Tears formed in Diana's eyes as she watched the beloved dragon's receding shape. She clung to the last scales, daring to open her hand enough to see the turquoise, ruby, and opalescent residues that painted her palm and dusted the golden-brown terra flakes, still intact. She snapped her hand closed, as if she could stop the ritual—stop things from changing—just by holding tightly to the terra scales.

Clarin soared over the treetops, clearing avocado and orange trees by a fraction of an inch, her sleek brown form upsetting the leaves. The Western Sphere emitted the final QuinKelling beacon. It resounded deep in her heartfire, allowing Clarin to navigate instinctively. Due west she flew. All but the ritual signal fell away, including her grief at the necessity of perilously dividing their family to create the critical haven of the QuinKell.

The sleek mother dragon crossed canyons and groves. The QuinKelling tone pulsed in time with her heart; her wing strokes beat in double time. The sphere was close.

At any other time, Clarin would feel the presence of any dragon nearby, but the lure of the QuinKelling blotted out all else. Still, Clarin's senses piqued. A shadow, subtle movement, a jostling of the brush caught her eye just below her right periphery. The beacon might block magical intuition, but not maternal. She slowed her flight suddenly and veered to the right. A smoky presence below her, sailing above the brush, matched her sudden deceleration, but too late to prevent detection. The hazy shape of a dragon—Gryn in terra invisibility form—became as unmistakable as if the dragon had been flying uncloaked. *Gryn!* Her daughter. *No!* thought the mother, her telepathy within the QuinKelling inaccessible, useless.

Gryn had crouched behind some nearby desert gorse just after the ritual had begun. Poised for invisibility and flight, she'd known the QuinKelling would blot out her presence to the other dragons, even their mother. When Clarin took off, Gryn burst into low flight,— unseen by Diana or her dragon siblings—and followed her mother, keeping stealthily behind her.

Clarin flew with all her maternal might. Sensing discovery, Gryn shed her disguise and used the extra energy to match her speeding mother. Clarin beat her wings with new-found fury as Gryn chased her. Gryn dove recklessly under reaching palms, around pointed yuccas; she pulled up and over a huge round boulder, clearing it by mere millimeters and scraping scales off her underbelly on some broken stone protruding from the top of the rock.

The two terras raced between the branches of the last few trees, cutting and scratching their backs and wings, neither feeling a thing. But Gryn was not quite a match for her mother's strength and experience. Just a few more seconds, and Clarin would pull ahead enough to lock her daughter out of the sacrifice.

Clarin sailed over the last rise before the Sphere. She burst through the feathery tops of the wild grass, leaving a lightning part through the stems, the long blades lying flat as though in homage to the mother's will. Gryn appeared at the edge of Clarin's vision, swooping so deftly that she brought herself nearly as close as her mother to the beckoning tower. Clarin put her head down and dove toward the goal with all she had. Her umber crest glowed in the sun as her will shot her forward. She was winning, the Sphere lay just beyond her feet.

The relief of her triumph rang through her: *She's free, she's free,* became her heartbeat. *My daughter, you are free...*

...became her last thought;

...before she fell;

...before paralysis;

...before blackness cloaked her in the comfort of unknowing.

From her speeding flight, the young terra saw her mother fall. Gryn ascended the kelling sphere, while her mother's wings froze and drooped and her body crashed the few feet to the ground. Clarin, immobilized, rolled away from the gleaming beacon and away from her daughter's salvation.

Gryn dodged the airspace her mother had last occupied and came around to the Sphere from the side. The young terra had dispersed dragondregs into her mother's path. The release from their protective casing caused Gryn to wobble in the air, but she had prepared for the effect and used a stunted burst of firebreath to aim the full blast of toxic dust just as she had designed: right into her mother's field of flight. As Gryn took her place, her only regret floated through her: knowing her mother would rue the gift.

Alone at the ritual's origination, Diana still cleaved to the last scales, a part of her hoping they would never dissolve, but knowing how disastrous this would be. The brown scale began to dissolve. She gripped it tightly, futile in her effort to keep it from leaving her. In another second, she opened her hand, prisms of color still clinging to her skin. Acquiescing to the inevitable, she raised her open palm and allowed the breeze to carry away the golden remnants. "Goodbye, Clarin," she whispered into the golden air. The tears that had held like a swelling river overran her, running down her cheeks, dropping heavily from her face onto the lonely ground.

Gryn became the fourth and last stone Sentinel, light like a sunrise enveloping her on the sphere. The strains of the QuinKell pledge left her, though Diana barely heard the words over her own sobs. The final transformation was nearly complete. Below, Clarin awakened and stood, desperately trying to drive away the delirium. But she looked up only in time to watch, helpless, as the final, fateful encasement swallowed the last living vestige of her daughter. Clarin's voice, the physical chords rarely called upon, uttered a woeful, dissonant cry that carried over the forest and died on the wind before any but the curious wildlife could hear. She flew up to the top of the sphere and regarded her brave, foolish, defiant daughter: Gryn was now a tiger's eye guardian, her wings folded, head looking up to the sky, her rich, shining presence rivaling the sun.

Clarin flew to a boulder outcropping adjacent to her daughter's enthronement. She had the company of birds and squirrels, even the insects, in regarding the magical beauty and stony stubbornness of their new desert guardian. In her disbelief and grief, she had no company. Clarin regained her strength to make the flight back to the others. She willed herself to fly quickly, feeling pulled and stretched as if by a rubber band threatening to snap as she flew away from her child. As the sudden, unexpected loss of her daughter clashed in her heart against the realization that she herself remained free, each strained upstroke and downstroke of her wings beat the cadence, *It should have been me; I can only accept it...*

~

In front of Diana, as Clarin had foretold, the mistcrystal, still burning in celestial radiance, began its rise. Diana released it to its destiny as her tears continued to flow. She raised her face to the path of the mistcrystal. Clasping her hands in front of her, she spread the traces of the scales across both hands, and then lifted her hands to her tear-streaked face, leaving a luminous rainbow smudging her cheeks.

The mistcrystal remained suspended above her head. Eyes still fixed on it, she placed her hands at her sides and tried to relax; she tried to follow Clarin's earlier directives. *I must give myself to the kelling.*

Her feet became magnetized to the ground. She felt as though a thin wire containing a new current from the mistcrystal ran through the top of her head, down the center of her body, and into the ground. It felt electric—cool and crisp—yet still electric.

A fountain of color, a rotating geyser of light, shot from the mistcrystal. Rather than look away from the blinding beam, Diana felt pulled toward it. Pressure within her chest built to a tight pain, as she felt her core gravitate toward the emanation of spinning light. Her feet were still joined to the energy traveling down, down, through the earth. She tensed everywhere at the conflicting pressures on her body and soul.

Her legs ached, her knees threatened to buckle. Her face broke out in sweat, darkening the smears of color on her cheeks. She felt her heart pound, felt it trying to fly from her chest to join the shaft of spectral lightning racing up to the clouds. *I can't do it*, she thought, the perspiration was joined by more tears that washed the shimmering scale dust almost completely away and spotted her khaki shirt in a mockery of beautiful hues.

Diana fell to her knees and hung her head, which only increased the pain in her chest as her bent skeleton fought against her heart's pull to join the light. She rocked back on stinging heels as the invisible wire grounding them stretched to its limits.

Then she heard Clarin's words again, the instructions before the ritual: *I'm sorry you'll feel the pain of this evocation. Whatever happens, let go. Submit to the QuinKell. Let yourself become a part of it.* Diana stopped fighting the various stresses compelling her. Breathing deeply, she tried to relax every muscle. Immediately, she felt the tensions ease. She took another breath, now able to fill her lungs to capacity. She felt like she was floating.

She looked down at her shoes; they still rested on the pebbly soil. But rather than feeling the hard desert land beneath the worn soles of her sneakers, she felt only the energy that connected her to the power of both the outflow of light and the round, deep earth. She inhaled again, and lightness of being inhabited her every cell. *I think I can feel the ends of my hair*, she thought.

Diana closed her eyes. Her mind drifted from one sensation to another, somehow peacefully aware of the enormity of the power flowing through her. She felt the follicles of the hairs on her arms, the pores in her skin, even the marrow in her bones. She felt the mighty light insider her, rather than in front of her. She remained still, time meaningless, as everything within her became creation.

Then, as if awaking from a dream, she opened her eyes. She felt her feet, felt the familiar weight of her own body on the ground.

The incandescence of the mistcrystal ceased in a loud clap, an exploding white dwarf in Diana's personal universe. The crystal was black. Diana, every sense sharpened, caught the dead-looking orb as it fell from its place in the air. She immediately dropped it, shaking her hand and wincing.

"Owww, it's freezing," she said to the empty air.

Diana fell to her knees and, with trepidation, reached down and touched the mistcrystal. It immediately returned to something closer to its usual light and churning fog. She picked it up and began to put it back around her neck, then paused and stared at the ground.

The spot where the mistcrystal had landed was no longer the normal green and brown scrub forest floor, but a black, fathomless hole in the ground the size of the crystal.

Chapter Twenty

Within the Birth of the QuinKell

Jake and Nicki stood on the porch at Diana's house. Dr. Kim's house was just a few blocks outside what would become the boundaries of the QuinKell. Dr. Kim and the sheriff would keep watch over Shay and the hatchlings.

"It's too bad they couldn't just make the QuinKell cover Dr. Kim's," Jake muttered.

"Yeah," Nicki sighed, "But I'm sure the dragons are right. We don't know what else Illsworth might have that could mess up the magic."

"I'd love to get my hands on that guy," Jake said through clenched teeth.

"Wouldn't we all," Nicki answered, her almond-shaped eyes narrowing. There was rare venom in her tone, something Jake had certainly never heard.

Nicki set up her video camera and had her phone charged for notes and pictures. Jake had brought a "real" camera his dad loaned him, and he offered it to the grateful Nicki, who actually had some clue how to use it.

Jake looked all around the skies. "What do you think it will feel like?" he asked, trying to sound brave.

"Nothing, I imagine," Nicki replied, trying to sound equally sure. "It's not like the air is changing or something." Her face contradicted her certainty. "There just won't be any bad magic."

"And a lot of the good kind," Jake added, smiling, somewhat convincing. "Diana said it would make a sort of bubble. Maybe it will feel like a big burp."

"Funny," Nicki said, a little grossed out, but she looked like she might be running it through her mind just for the distraction of it.

"Look!" Jake cried. "Look at that!"

"What? What is it?" a small voice shouted through the screen door. Brody got louder, calling back into the house, "Mom, come on! Please can I go out now?"

Mrs. Santos brought her son to the porch, standing with her back to the door and his shoulders in her grip.

"Mom!" The boy tried to pull away.

"I'm not worried about the QuinKell," she explained, mostly meaning it, her eyes traveling around the yard. "I'm worried about

Illsworth," she said, though Sheriff Gonzales had officers watching him. "So just stay close."

"Um...that doesn't look like anything good," Nicki said in an intense, but restrained, tone. And since there was not a sound anywhere—no birds, no planes, no wind—the others heard her as clearly as if they'd said it themselves. Jake remained pointing at a spot in the sky where a light beam appeared from nowhere, a spinning barbershop pole of blurring colors. More light, subtly colored and constantly changing, fanned out from the shaft of light like flowers from a magician's wand. A contagious shiver seemed to pass between Jake and Nicki, as goosebumps appeared all over both of them.

"I wish we could touch it," Brody said, approaching the bannister. His mother followed, though she remained focused on the incredible sight. Billowing up from the blossoming light, magical threads stretched and bent to create a tapestry of interwoven hues.

A blanket of light formed above them: a giant, pastel square of kaleidoscopic transparency, like a vaporous parachute drifting down over the sky. And they were right under one of its corners.

"It's amazing," Nicki said, camera shutter clicking. "Here." She handed Jake her phone with the camera already set.

"Yeah, it is...So why do I feel like we should duck?" He took a few pictures, stopping here and there to rub the goosebumps on his arms. "It's actually kinda creeping me out," Jake went on, as the dog next to them began to bark, causing them both to jump.

"It's OK, Aggie," Mrs. Santos soothed, while Brody knelt to pet their old border collie.

"I bet this is what she feels like right before an earthquake," Nicki remarked, her heart beating quicker as she tried to sound calm. They all now regarded the dog, who, a moment before, had been lying at their feet, sound asleep. She stood with her paws on the porch rail and wagged her tail vigorously, pointing her nose toward the epicenter of the phenomenon. Stretching her head over the porch railing, she seemed to be trying to sniff in the whole of the odd occurrence.

"Jeez, she looks more like she does when I dangle a piece of jerky in front of her," Jake said, amazed.

"I know. So happy..." Nicki trailed off quietly. She and Jake instinctively joined Brody in stroking the dog's fur. Linda stood with her hand resting lightly on her son's messy hair. They all grew quiet and watched, as from the rainbow core, the sky-shawl continued to settle. They watched as it began to change the very air.

Cars on the neighborhood roads stopped, the engines and radios simply quitting in unison. Everything paused, the wildlife grew still; all were aimed toward the center of the erupting QuinKell. People got out of their cars. If mothers and fathers feared for their children, their instinctive embraces yielded nothing but stillness and serenity as the children, too, faced the event. Those in valleys, behind hills, or in buildings, who could not directly view the burgeoning haze, came out anyway and automatically aligned their gazes toward its advent.

Jake, Nicki, Linda Santos, and even Brody stood mesmerized, as the soft fibers of light settled around the borders of the QuinKell. "Look!" Jake cried, as the ends of the twinkling quilt of near-nothingness slid down the sky. The edges touched down and merged into the grass and plants near the boundary of Diana's yard, meeting the ground with a momentary reaction, like a puff of dust kicked up by a heavy object, but the "dust" was made of light and color.

"Wow," Nicki said, putting down the camera and running toward the settling shroud, Aggie on her heels. Aggie ran to the veil of dusk and poked her head right through.

"Aggie, get ba—" Jake started, running up right behind them, then broke off, eyes wide. "You have to see this," he called to Mrs. Santos, who then ran out with Brody.

They all stared, dumbstruck. They stared some more, incredulity turning to bliss. They could see a sharp, faint—yet clearly visible—line across Aggie's neck. The dog's black fur was duller and dimmer where it protruded *outside* the envelope of beguiling brilliance.

~

Knowing her house and the dragon den below fell outside the QuinKell, Dr. Kim and the sheriff were on high alert, more so than in the previous weeks, since such an unprecedented occurrence was at hand. It would be the first order of business to move Shay and the hatchlings—and poor little Phaed's shiftcrystal—to the QuinKell.

Dr. Kim stood on her front steps, Sheriff Gonzales in the yard, both looking toward the area they knew would be engulfed in the magic. Dr. Kim had never been so excited, curious, and alarmed all at once. She called to Max, "If I knew any DEFCON statuses, I'd set us to the top color."

"Let's just stay on our toes," came back Max's calming baritone as he scanned the road, the edges of the yard, and checked in on the radio with the officers he had around the perimeter. None of them had any idea what or who they were guarding, or from what or whom, just that they were ordered to watch for suspicious activity. Most likely, the biggest problem would come from the rightfully curious and possibly frightened public. Max was prepared to set up a road block and cite the amorphous reason of "public safety," if necessary. If and when the calls flooded in for the sheriff, Dr. Kim had a local T.V. reporter at the ready to broadcast the breaking story to explain the inexplicable. It was her dearest hope that the public would be held at bay until the dragons and Phaed's shiftcrystal—dangerous while there and unburied—were safely ensconced in their lair within the QuinKell.

About an hour after the sheriff had talked a deputy out of believing he'd just seen an "albino hawk or something stranger" flying north on the horizon, it began. From outside the QuinKell, the light and color show took on a deeper intensity and contrast. As soon as the light-bearing column appeared in the sky, the law officers' radios sparked up. Sheriff Gonzales ordered them to keep their positions, assuring them that there was no cause for alarm. A few more transmissions of questioning and disbelief transpired, then silence. Each person witnessing the eruption of the QuinKell's brilliance, a few hundred yards from their location, stood in awe.

Dr. Kim walked out to join Max. "It's magnificent."

"Unbelievable," said the lawman.

"Look." Dr. Kim pointed as the resulting blanket of light reached the only squared border they could see from their vantage point. "It's just draping over an edge in the sky like a tablecloth." They gaped like children at the bending array of light, which looked immaterial and material all at once.

"Well, I'll be. The sky..." the sheriff paused, staring out in wonder, "...the sky has a corner," he concluded, his baritone raspy.

"It does, indeed," said Dr. Kim, "a beautiful, impossible, completely undeniable corner."

The sheriff checked in with his officers, careful not to give too much information away. It became obvious that neither they nor the general public had *quite* witnessed the event. One officer, Deputy Bandy, who knew something highly irregular—not exactly what— was up, reported, "The people in town just all seem to be in a really good mood." It was like everyone in proximity to the occurrence was enjoying a beautiful sunset they hadn't actually seen. The sheriff sent several officers to patrol the roads, talked with the guard observing Illsworth, and kept his own watch around the house.

Inside the basement dragon den, it was pandemonium—happy pandemonium—but pandemonium nonetheless. Dr. Kim ran down the stairs, beckoned by constant little taps and clanks. She arrived in the den to see eleven dragonlings jumping and hopping and attempting to fly, all drawn to the direction of the QuinKell. Shay watched his children with the eye of an amused but alert parent ready to intervene should the mirth upset more than just a few clay pots. The dragonlings piled upon one another on the far ledge, feeling the draw of the Quinkell through the western wall.

Dr. Kim looked at Shay, and in him saw both the pride of parenthood and the sorrow of loss. She pulled out a stool they had pushed under the stairs to make way for the increased activity of the developing brood and sat near the father dragon. She placed her hand on his fore-talon and held it there, watching his children with him and sighing intermittently in the knowledge that the only comfort for Shay lay in just being with him and helping him with these children he'd created with Clarin.

Finally, Dr. Kim, tears brimming, breathed out her only spoken consolation, "I'm so sorry about your children," Dr. Kim's voice caught, "and Clarin." She blinked away tears as she saw the frosty buildup in the corners of Shay's eyes, the naked manifestation of the cold of his grief.

~

The QuinKelling beacon ceased. The ritual was complete. Miles across, the impenetrable shroud would protect the dragons and all who entered. As the frequencies continued to settle, discordant intentions would dissipate as any

262

creature passed through the ethereal membrane, inviting harmonious thought and action within the QuinKell. What the dragonkin had evolved among themselves over millennia could exist here in this space, as long as the dragon-gem sentries remained. And they, the Sentinels, were reflectively protected by the magic they had evoked with their sacrifice.

Diana still stood in the center space, holding the mistcrystal, her tears beginning to ebb. New vibrations pulsed through the mistcrystal, nothing like the normal frequency that always connected her to Clarin. Yet, somehow, she was far from alarmed.

She felt herself surrender to the orchestrations of the QuinKell. Her drying tears reminded her of the loss of Clarin and the other dragons, as the emerging vibrations within the new atmosphere began to make room within her for acceptance. She began to walk north, knew she must leave the QuinKell, get to Dr. Kim's; she had to help move the dragons and the shiftcrystal. Diana ran. It was over a quarter mile to Dr. Kim's, and her cell phone would not work within the QuinKell. She wanted to be with the rest of the dragons and her family and friends as soon as possible.

Diana saw the outside world darkly through the veil toward which she ran, stepped through, and looked back—Alice exiting Wonderland—and the buoyancy of its effects began to subside. She took out her phone and texted everyone, then picked back up her jog. Within a few steps, the sadness crept in. *Clarin,* she thought, and the tears welled. She ran. *Clarin, what will I do—what will* we *do without you*? She thought of her father. The emptiness left by the sacrifice of Clarin and her children; the gaping void created by the long absence of her father: these realities tumbled together inside her. Tears began to roll from her eyes. She ran faster, trying to fill the desolation with the pounding of her steps. She cried freely, the tears now blurring her vision. If only they could blur her sorrow.

Diana glimpsed Dr. Kim's house through the sparse trees and ran down a gully and up the rise on the other side to see the house even larger. She ran until her chest might burst. *Daddy*, her heart cried. *Clarin*, she thought desperately, as she reached the edge of the yard. As she slowed, the sadness overwhelmed her. She sank down on the grass.

The sheriff was coming toward her. Somewhere close by, a car engine sputtered.

Diana's senses were obscured in her tears and loss. She sat holding her knees and cried into her crossed arms, the dragon scale dust running from her face. The sheriff's black shoes appeared next to her. The noise of the car engine had ceased. She tried to stop sobbing. "Daddy," she said aloud, "Clarin." Her mother, baby brother, and friends were coming toward her while the sheriff stood by her. *Clarin...Clarin...*Diana thought over and over and continued to cry. "Oh, Clarin—"

Yes, Diana.

"Clarin?" Diana stood and shouted, "Clarin!" The others stared at her, her mother coming to her side, as if to support her daughter in her unsound mind. Diana shook her off and looked to the skies, to the QuinKell.

As the QuinKell beacon had subsided in Clarin's heartfire, she had called out to Diana, hoping to reach her within the QuinKell, hoping to spare her the pain. The frequencies within the new QuinKell drifted within their framework, chaotic strains still composing themselves into order. She had not been able to find Diana telepathically through the confusion. So she had flown to find her.

Diana heard the salvational voice again, *Diana, I'm here. I'm still with you.* Diana's tears overflowed, now with laughter and joy. She turned to everyone else. "She's here. She's still here!"

They all started asking questions at once. Diana waved them away as she busily searched the sky. There, over the trees, glowing golden brown, chest crests sparkling in the twilight, flying straight for her, was Clarin. She landed inches from Diana, folded her wings to her side, and received Diana's embrace. Everyone gathered around. Diana released her hold, then looked into Clarin's eyes, as Clarin allowed Diana to be privy to the thoughts the dragon shared with Shay: *Yes, my beloved. I'm coming.* Then, in a somber tone: *Yes, our daughter. All four made the sacrifice.*

They went to the basement den to reunite the dragon family. When Clarin met Shay, she tucked herself beneath his strong chest, their heartfires glowing as one. The little brood flowed over like candy-colored lava, fitting themselves into the nooks and crannies under and between the dragon couple. Diana and the others took one long look and headed silently up to the first floor, pulling the black curtain over the window to give the dragons utter stillness and peace for their last night in their first home among their humankin.

~

A thousand feet away, Illsworth stood at one of his massive windows, the rarely opened curtains pulled back fully. He regarded the pastel-polished sky, turning the shiftcrystal in his hand. Next to him, with white light glaring from behind, Ayan strained at his tethers, his sickly, transparent scales falling where the chains bit at his limbs. With his whole body he yearned, reached, and stretched to the limit of the chains, everything in the tortured ghost pulling him toward the QuinKell.

Chapter Twenty-One

Escape to the QuinKell

Behind heavy guard and with the sheriff's deputies monitoring Illsworth under the semi-truth of suspicion of poaching, Diana, the dragons, and the extended humankin slept under one roof. In a blur of emotion and discussion, food was eaten, stories were traded, dragonlings were played with. And dragons were missed. Mourning for the lost and sacrificed dragons added a layer of aching to the foundations of every activity.

While the nearby QuinKell's mystic airwaves arranged themselves, the dragons and humankin dared not expose the dragonlings to the unfinished array. Clarin made it quite clear that such ancient magic brought with it many unknowns. They would wait until Clarin and Shay—and Diana via the mistcrystal—could feel the safe invitation to inhabit.

The party had discussed the mystery still surrounding Diana's father while sitting around the sun-streaked basement den, everyone interacting here and there with a frolicking baby dragon. The hatchlings were now about seven inches long and old enough to inhibit their firebreath, especially with a squelching admonishment from a parent. Soon they would be of age to be named.

Jeff Santos, Clarin was sure, was being prevented from returning by the same source that supplied Illsworth with his stolen dragon knowledge and power. Clarin and Shay shared the grief of the loss of their children, their hearts closer through the pain and in the belief that the sacrifices served the highest good for all, even those now lost. Shay lamented that he might have prevented Gryn from tricking him into believing she simply wanted to take flight to help her cope with losing her siblings to the QuinKell. He was met with unconditional understanding by Clarin. If only it were not so easy for this gifted new terra to choose which thoughts to keep quiet. Another nature would need much more growth and experience to shield such ideations from a father dragon.

No one could bear to leave, save Sheriff Gonzales, who had the guard duties to which to attend, so Dr. Kim set up the living room and guest room for sleeping.

"We have to do it today," Diana said aloud, sitting up with a jolt and throwing the sleeping bag off of her onto Nicki's sleeping face.

"Of course we do," Dr. Kim said, looking into the living room from the kitchen. She had been awake since before dawn. Nicki stirred and immediately started to get up and stow the bedding. "Leave it," Dr. Kim said with a dismissive wave. Jake and Brody came from down the hall, where Jake had volunteered to sleep, and Brody had insisted he camp out, too. Linda came out of the guest room and ushered Brody into whatever rudiments of grooming she could persuade him to perform.

"It's time," Diana said, to herself and to everyone. Mrs. Santos shared a look of "here we go again" with Dr. Kim.

"Come on," Diana commanded as she headed for the basement, her mistcrystal enlivened like the day the dragons returned, but with a stronger, fuller rhythm, practically a hum.

"Look at it," Nicki marvelled, reaching for the stone and hesitating for a moment before Diana nodded and shrugged the go-ahead. As Nicki lifted it slightly, everyone in the room could see the added luminosity and depth of color. It still looked like Clarin's golden brown mist, but now it burned as well.

"Just beautiful," Linda said while everyone nodded in agreement. "I wish Jeff could see it," she added quietly. They filed down to the basement to find the dragons awake and waiting. Brody sat on the dusty floor in front of Clarin's perch, as two seas hopped into the triangle where the boy sat cross-legged. Each dragon jumped into the air, blowing a silly puff of steam in his face, then floated down on unsure wings to repeat the fun.

Brody rubbed his face and laughed. "They smell like the dryer when the clothes are still wet."

Clarin's thoughts came to Diana, who related them, "Tynan, Merac, Tethys, and Gryn are lost indefinitely, and we know you share our deep desire that no more loss be tolerated." Everyone nodded. Diana continued her translation, paraphrasing, "Inside the QuinKell, we may find out more about Dad's predicament." At this Diana and Clarin both looked to Mrs. Santos, who was gazing at her small son, happy he was entranced by the dragons at this moment.

Linda Santos looked at her daughter, who continued to repeat the mother dragon's thoughts: "Of course we must get the hatchlings there as quickly as possible."

Diana, eyes down, added, "And bury Phaed's shiftcrystal as soon as we can."

Jake piped up, "Illsworth's already got one..."

The party all nodded.

"He'll want to get his hands on this one, too," Dr. Kim said, gesturing toward the cold little orb.

"My dad said he and Deputy Sullivan have seen Illsworth pacing his yard, staring out the windows, and hardly ever leaving his grounds since you rescued the dragons from his house," Jake said.

"Since *we* rescued the dragons," Diana corrected. She looked at Jake's arms, still bandaged, some of the scratches now fine lines crossing his arms and hands.

Nicki had been staring at the baby terra who was taking in huge breaths, wrapping her arms around a shed scale, and glowing an adorable burnt-orange in her tiny face as she tried to direct the firebreath to travel to all of her scales. Nicki interjected, "Can Ayan be helped with the firesaving?"

Clarin's answer, spoken through Diana was a gentle, "I believe he can. Of course I must try to help my son. If we can get him out."

Diana looked at her friend a little sideways. She saw Nicki had *that look* and asked her, almost sounding suspicious, "Why?" Her quiet friend, who had seemed not to be paying attention, let a few seconds go by, her brain ticking along.

Finally, Nicki said, "Well, we need to save Ayan. And we have what Illsworth wants."

The whole party looked around, taking in the scattered, busy dragonlings and the nest area, now a messy expanse of loose straw, petite claw prints, and little black patches of char. Among the scatterings lay the collection of eleven radiant, motile mistcrystals and the static, white shiftcrystal bisected by the terrible blood-red line.

Diana picked up on Nicki's lead. "He wants all the dragons and everything related to them." At this, Brody attempted to scoop the seas up into his lap, as well as a little sun, who was flapping its wings in an attempt to ascend the heights of Brody's crossed legs.

"And as we've noted," Dr. Kim said, looking at Nicki and raising an eyebrow, "he really wants Phaed's shiftcrystal." Nicki nodded vigorously.

"And for who knows what," Mrs. Santos said softly, her eyes turned toward the small window.

Diana spoke Clarin's thoughts again, "Clarin says she must transport the shiftcrystal herself."

"We can lure Ayan, I bet," Nicki said, though quietly, as if she wanted to take back her idea as soon as she shared it.

"But the hatchlings!" Brody cried, as he imagined the big, messed-up dragon attacking the cute little dragons.

Clarin assured them through Diana, "We will not expose the hatchlings to Ayan while he is under this influence."

Diana turned to Jake. "Can you ask your dad to help us with this stuff?" Jake called his dad, who said he was already on his way back over.

Everyone took a little break to do normal things, except Diana, who sat on the floor with Brody and let the dragon babies climb all over her. The terra jumped off the ledge, established a more-or-less graceful float and single wingstroke, and landed on Diana's calf where it perched to examine the girl who wore its mother's mistcrystal. Clarin looked at them, and Diana heard, *I knew you two would get along.*

Once reassembled, the humankin and dragon parents plotted and prepared for hours, setting their plan for twilight. Outside to the east, the QuinKell stood, a steady invitation to enter its realm—an invitation much local wildlife had already accepted. Birds filled the trees, their continuous songs overlapping. Deer, raccoons, and coyotes from the surrounding land were also drawn to the space. Owls swooped near their frolicking prey, but for this night, they left the scurrying creatures alone, content to soar through the sky and perch beneficently on the green branches of oaks that somehow seemed fuller.

~

Illsworth ran his rough, pale hand over the worn wooden box, lingering over the ouroboros carved into the top. He opened the box, removed the from his hand the heavy silver ring set with the shiftcrystal, and placed it on the strange, luminescent lining. He closed the box and exited the dimly lit room, heading for the now dragonless dragon prison. With the eerie floodlights off, the room was cold and gray, the floor an antiseptic white tile, the fixtures stainless steel—a surgery suite in which none were healed. He opened a drawer and removed several black boxes of varying sizes, each bearing the ouroboros.

The only men on the property that day were those who had defended against the theft of his captives. These he initiated into just enough knowledge to enlist their proper service. One of the brutes lay in wait outside the new interference erected by the dragons, waiting to signal Illsworth of any movement. Illsworth walked from the sterile torture chamber to the quarters where he held Ayan. The dragon lay on the cold floor, twitching in a fitful sleep. Still assaulting him was the menacing light array, set to the lowest level Illsworth permitted for the dragon to regenerate. The ghost had fallen asleep while still straining toward the allure of the QuinKell.

Illsworth turned up the brightness of the lights. The dragon stirred, his head wobbling, and attempted to stand, but was pulled back to the floor by the short chain. Illsworth bent and hung a small box around the dragon's neck. He petted the sickly creature on the head, his touch the patronizing threat of a heartless master.

~

"Get your shoes on, " Linda Santos said for the third time, advancing on her son to complete the shoeing herself.

"I don't want to go!" Brody whined. Mrs. Santos was taking Brody into town to drop him off with friends.

"I have to know you are safe when all this is happening," his mom said, speaking softly but pushing his second shoe on firmly.

He protested, "But Mommy, Diana said the *quin-kelly* thing is the safest place."

"Yes, honey. I believe that. But it's better if you're a few miles away until everything is settled." Brody looked at his mother from where he hunched down on the couch. He wore a frustrated but acquiescing grimace. "I'll come get you as soon as the dragons are safely in the hideaway." His face cleared a bit, then fell back into a frown.

Sheriff Gonzales popped his head out of the kitchen and coaxed, "Hey, how about when everything's squared away, I come pick you up in the sheriff's car?"

"Awesome!" Brody said, and with a slightly less longing look around, let his mother bustle him out the door.

Nicki had run to Dr. Kim's storage in the garage. She came back with two animal crates and ran back for two more. She left two in the kitchen and took two to the basement.

Dusk fell. Diana, Clarin, the sheriff, and Nicki left from the side door. Sheriff Gonzales carried the two crates, glimpses of something bright and colorful showing through the tiny metal bars set in the plastic. Clarin paused at a fallow flower bed to dig into the soil, casting Diana's elementor onto her claws and stretching it out for Diana to accept. Once the wings adhered, she and the dragon took flight.

In the garage, Dr. Kim, Jake, and Mrs. Santos finished packing her small, black SUV. Shay, the last one in, crouched in the back of the cargo space between the equipment, two crates, and the tailgate. They left a convincing number of lights on in the house and the blinds and curtains closed. Then they sat in the vehicle in the dark with the engine off, and waited.

~

Nicki and the sheriff had been walking east for about half an hour, the two flyers circling in reconnaissance above them, when Clarin spotted Illsworth's stooge. Lying beneath some brush, his camouflage was no match for the dragon's vision or intuition. Clarin barreled toward the man and blasted amber fire a few feet in front of his petrified face. He scrambled back, stumbled through the shrubs, and ran. Clarin and Diana flew to the others, touching down briefly so Diana could report the encounter.

"He'll be calling Illsworth," Nicki said.

"That's what we're counting on," answered the sheriff. Over his police radio, he checked in with the deputies staked out at Illsworth's and on the road outside the QuinKell. Though the deputies had no idea of the magical component, they took poaching very seriously and stood ready with any means necessary to halt such violators. "Let's go," he said and led the way. Nicki walked by his side, flashlight in her hand and a full pack slung onto her back.

In the trees between the trekkers and the QuinKell, fifty vultures perched, unseen specks against the darkening sky.

Clarin had taken flight again. Diana walked next to Nicki and the sheriff for a few paces,

Diana's elementor bouncing against her back, shining in with golden streaks in the dark like her hair did in the sun. "I wish I had paid attention to how long it took to run from the QuinKell," she said.

"You had a lot on your mind," said Nicki. She picked up her pace to keep up with the sheriff. Diana took off, scouring the skies, her vision no better with the mistcrystal, but she navigated by the dragon's lead. Clarin thought, obviously responding to Shay, *We're fine. We will hide the shiftcrystal and come back for you.*

Another of Illsworth's men lurked just yards from the sheriff and Nicki. Clarin caught sight of him and swooped down as Diana was pulled to follow. Diana shouted to the sheriff as Clarin screeched her rare, vocalized warning. Setting the carriers down, Sheriff Gonzales pulled out his gun, guiding Nicki behind him. She shone the light toward the trees and caught a glimpse of the green-shirted thug. In his hands was a rope, from which dangled a black container. He began to swing the box like a sling. "Diana!" Nicki screamed, too late. Tiny, glittery particles trailed through the air from an opening in the box, right into Diana's and Clarin's paths.

As if slammed around a tetherball pole, Diana and Clarin catapulted in an arc with enormous force. Diana was hurled into the sharp and stinging branches of an oak, where she landed with a thud as her stomach collided with the thickest horizontal branch. Semi-conscious, her limp body lay draped over the branch, bleeding arms dangling.

Clarin slammed into a boulder on a hill and slid, unconscious, to the ground. As her head hit the ground, the shiftcrystal she protected—a mother dragon's solitary task before burial—was dislodged from the pouch in her cheek. It rolled away from her to disappear under the fallen oak leaves.

Nicki, horrified, still remembered her role. Sheltered by the sheriff, she sent the pre-written text to the waiting group. In Dr. Kim's garage, the three phones lit up simultaneously. With her headlights off and garage door light disconnected, Dr. Kim rolled out of the driveway and sped down the road toward the QuinKell. At an unobservable distance, a second, unlit car pulled out from the brush next to the house and followed in the dark.

Diana came to almost immediately and slid out of the branches, which scratched and cut her as she gracelessly dropped the five feet to the ground. She ran to Clarin, nearby shouts hitting her ears like clanging bells, unintelligible. Diana felt her throat start to close. She stooped over Clarin's motionless form. She bent so that her cheek was in front of Clarin's jaw.

The dragon's breath was dangerously cool. *Oh, no,* her mind cried. Diana felt paralyzed. More shouts reached her ears. She spun and shielded Clarin with her body, the undamaged elementor swinging behind her. An industrial powered flashlight beam landed in her eyes, followed by Nicki's face behind it, distorted by the bobbing light and terror. "Diana, are you alright?" Nicki put the light out and sat with Diana, her back toward her friend and the dragon, ready to react to the shouts between the sheriff and Illsworth's creepy assailant. Nicki's presence brought Diana's heart rate down a few beats. Nicki pulled the elucifier from her backpack and shined it on Clarin. The dragon opened her eyes. Diana's mistcrystal warmed and began to increase in motion.

"Here," Diana said, and aided the dragon in her attempt to stand.

A shot rang out. Then another. "Girls, go!" the sheriff shouted, just before another gun blast. Nicki shined the light toward the noise.

Diana and Clarin were up. The three looked into the path of the light to see the dark sky falling—falling in pieces of beaks and feathers— and descending on the sheriff.

Stay on the ground, Clarin warned Diana, as she took flight, shaking a little as her feet left the earth. Diana and Nicki ran toward the sheriff. Some of the birds were attracted to the light, so while Nicki swung her beam away from the sheriff, Diana grabbed Nicki's pack and nearly ripped it off her, reaching in to find a second, enormous flashlight. She joined Nicki in waving the birds off the sheriff and the carriers.

~

On the road, Dr. Kim sped along at a speed quite far above her comfort level for the amount of moonlight guiding their non-head-lit path. Linda held fast to the passenger grip above the door, white knuckled but glad for the speed, while Jake sat rigid in the back seat, his hand on the equipment next to him, eyes peeled.

They heard the shots. Dr. Kim let up on the gas pedal momentarily. "Don't stop," Linda said, surprised at her resolve, reminding Dr. Kim of the plan and their promises to stick to it. Jake grabbed the seat back and squeezed, pulling his body forward as if he could propel the car with his momentum. In the back, Shay heard his mate's thoughts go silent. He tapped on the glass and Dr. Kim hit the button to lower the back window. Shay perched on the tailgate and launched himself into the night air with all his muscular might, pumping his wings hard. He pulled up from the rolling blacktop just in time, grazing his back talons on the road. Not daring to venture far from the car, he circled, his sea's vision the sharpest of that of any of the dragon natures. As another shot rang out, he banked toward the source and spotted the frenetic beams of light. He swooped around and buzzed the moving SUV, sweeping the area in front and to the sides for signs of movement. Satisfied, he dropped to a low flight path and began slowly and cautiously to move back toward the disturbance as one, two, three more shots perforated the night. He did not know why he couldn't hear his mate. Shay flew higher, where he saw an undulating line of black descending, a starless void replacing the deepening blue. *The vultures*, he thought, as the impulse to fly toward the onslaught gripped him.

No, my love, he heard. His mate's voice once again filled his mind, *Stay the course. They have dragondregs. We are drawing them closer to this side of the QuinKell. Keep going, my Shay.*

Shay doubled back to fly in front of the car. Led by the sea and his acute sight, Dr. Kim steered onto the tiny gravel trail that would lead them to the QuinKell faster than if they had taken the paved way that crossed Rolling Road and led to Diana's house. She slowed and flipped on her fog lights. Shay flew ahead of the car, swaying to and fro in its path to watch for dangers on the periphery. In the car, the carriers shook with the vibrations from the rut-filled road.

"There!" Linda pointed as the unmistakeable veil of the QuinKell appeared in front of them.

"Just a few dozen yards more," said Dr. Kim, with a slight increase in speed. Jake remained quiet, his eyes sweeping anything and everything in his limited sight lines.

Lightning shot at them from the side, obliterating Linda's window. "Get down!" Dr.

Kim yelled, but kept the car steady. An apparition appeared in front of Dr. Kim's windshield, before a screeching knot of wings and claws tumbled over the hood of the SUV. Dr. Kim hit the brakes, sending the carriers sliding to thump against the back of the seat amidst a protest of squawks and bellows.

Jake grabbed the object next to him, flipped the switch, and jumped out. In the front, Linda guided the cord over the seat, being sure to provide enough slack to keep it connected to the power source on the dashboard. Dr. Kim drove at a snail's pace, with Jake running alongside.

Ayan shot more fire and lightning at the car, lighting up the bumper and scorching the brush around the front of the vehicle like flashing mines. Shay rounded on his son, knocking him with his body to ruin the ghost's deadly aim before it could reach the boy. Jake took aim with the powerful floodlight he carried, sliding the beam back and forth in the sky, searching for the attacking dragon. Ayan had turned to face his father and was about to let loose a bolt, when Jake landed the superbeam directly in the ghost's face. At that, the dragon screeched and spread his wings like a phoenix, and the black box on his chest burst open to release a flurry of his own dragondregs. Shay careened backward and tumbled into the grass.

Across the canyon, Clarin heard Shay's desperate cry. She uttered a harrowing reply and flew toward her mate, his pain her navigation. The dragon's call sent chills of fear through Diana, who thought, *Ayan will kill his father. Ayan will kill them all.*

Sheriff Gonzales had Illsworth's man in his line of sight. "Stop right there," called the lawman, while Nicki continued to distract the birds from the ground and Diana from a hover in the air. The man ran away, toward the QuinKell. The sheriff chased after him, fending off vultures with his nightstick. Just as Max Gonzales was grabbing for the adversary's shirt, the man threw himself across the border of the QuinKell, his body rolling roughly to a stop on the ground where he lay motionless but for his gasping breath. Sheriff Gonzales abandoned his pursuit and ran toward the girls. The vultures were flying off in formation toward the direction of the car. One or two lay on the ground. Diana shouted, "I'm going!" and flew after the birds, ignoring the sheriff's protest.

"Nicki, your pack!" shouted the sheriff, and Nicki grabbed it off the ground, stumbling in the stream of light she cast in front of herself. The sheriff was pulling the devices off the dead vultures—three of them. He threw them into the bag as she opened it, then he zipped it up and put it on his own back. They abandoned the decoycarrier filled with Brody's beanbag toys and ran after Diana, guided by her beam in the sky as well as the lights and horrific noises from the battle beyond.

Dr. Kim's car inched forward as Ayan concentrated his fury on it. Jake ran to Shay and felt for his breath: too cool, but he breathed. Frightened at the prospect of trying the light that had seemed to backfire so horrendously with the burst of dragondregs, he froze. But it was his only option, so he forced himself to try again. Rather than subdue him at all, the light seemed to infuriate Ayan further. The dragon shot toward Jake like a torpedo. Jake knelt in front of Shay and hurled the metal light at the dragon, striking his left wing, but to little effect. Ayan bared his fangs, electricity visibly charging, his mouth a dark cavern flashing with an internal lightning storm. Jake watched in terror, throwing his arms up in futile resistance.

A golden, laser-like beam of firebreath struck Ayan from above. Clarin descended on her misguided child, driving him to the ground and covering him with her wings. He struggled, pushing at his mother, trying to shed the apron of leaden determination. His strength was supernatural, far too much to expect from any dragon in its natural state. He cast his mother's weight away, rising from their position in a nearly vertical take off.

Mrs. Santos jumped out of the door of the car, which Dr. Kim was still driving forward by inches whenever the way seemed momentarily clear. She shouted to Jake, "Get in!" motioning feverishly to the door she now held open.

Jake ran over gesturing back to her and shouting, "I'll get in the back!" Linda dove back into the car through the side door. Jake jumped in the back window, and Dr. Kim rolled it up after him. Settling next to the crates of shining, distressed dragonlings, he threw his arms around the crates and exclaimed, "It's OK. Your parents have got this!"

The QuinKell was yards away. Dr. Kim shot forward the moment the fighting dragons cleared the space in front of the vehicle, Clarin still raining warning breaths onto her son. With every discharge, the mother dragon cringed with heartbreak.

The front tires, half melted, carried the car bumping toward salvation. The dragons battled behind them. Ayan turned abruptly to chase the vehicle, his target the back window. Clarin raced her child, her only chance a blast of firebreath that would most certainly wound the confused dragon terribly. She narrowed the gap and inhaled. Ayan let loose a crack of lightning that shattered the back glass. Jake turned away, his back to the flying pieces, sheltering the crates of dragonlings with his body.

Just as Clarin was about to unleash the grieved firebreath, a figure flew from the side, careening into Ayan and sending him reeling in the air. He recovered and aimed his assault at his attacker: Diana. The crazed dragon rounded on Diana, and though not yet oriented well enough to aim properly, began spitting electricity onto Diana's arms, head, and body as he moved in for the critical bombardment. At that moment, Shay, recovered from the power of the dragondregs explosion, appeared on the other side of Ayan and knocked his son again, continuing the pounding with his forefeet and head until the ghost son was grounded.

Go with the others! Clarin ordered Diana. *Do not look back.* Diana couldn't resist and faltered on her magical wings as she looked down to see Clarin once again cover her son with her body, trying to get her wings positioned around him to perform the firesaving. Diana hesitated above the disastrous family reunion, then flew to the car and led the way in front of it. She crossed into the QuinKell. As she passed through the sheath of welcoming light, the SUV right behind her, relief filled her. She landed in front of the car as it limped to a stop and looked into the faces of the heroes inside.

The main venue of vultures had disappeared over the horizon. Where the mother and father dragon struggled with their son, a thinned but menacing flock began to lower. Shay broke away from Ayan and Clarin to fend off the birds, most of which retreated, completely spent. From the ominous boxes—worn by the few still in pursuit—trailed their last bits of dragondregs, just enough to sap some of the father dragon's powers. Shay flew unsteadily back toward Clarin, who felt her mate's depletion. She redoubled her efforts, but a few of the vultures followed Shay and another release of the dragondregs consumed some of her power. She began to lose her hold on Ayan.

~

Sheriff Gonzales and Nicki ran toward the QuinKell, a football field away from where the others had just delivered the vulnerable hatchlings. Shots rang through the night as the sheriff continued to fire into the flock. The scavengers scattered only briefly and then flew again toward him and Nicki. "Run!" he shouted to her, pointing to the glimmering boundary dividing the air. Nicki ran, her lungs nearly bursting. A few vultures pecked at her hair and flailing arms. Jake and Diana rushed toward the shots, Jake running and Diana flying low and fast. She saw Nicki and the sheriff outside the soft light of the QuinKell. She flew out of the boundary of the haven and hurled herself at the birds. Several vultures bit at her feet with their sharp beaks as she deftly shot upward to avoid them. She had drawn most of the birds away from Nicki. Diana circled back and flew above her. A few vultures followed as Nicki crossed into the QuinKell and fell to the ground, not seriously harmed. Jake ran to her side. The vultures inside the QuinKell gave up their chase immediately and veered up and away, flying in a lazy circle before landing gracefully in the trees.

Sheriff Gonzales ran through the boundary after Nicki, and finally the thunder of gunfire ceased. Diana took off again, heading for Clarin and Shay, who were still outside the safe haven. Shay deterred the cruel birds while Clarin wrestled their son until she was able to exude one firesaving breath onto him. Ayan succumbed to his mother; but, in his strange state he collapsed upon receiving the healing breath, cooling to the brink of lifelessness. Clarin and Shay picked up their child and flew him into the QuinKell, while Diana followed, covering them against the black specks that pursued them to the edge.

~

Illsworth examined the ground. He sprinkled an amber substance—it looked like liquid sparks—around the area, watching for a reaction. Several vultures perched above him in a low tree. His pale hand spread another dusting and there it was: an incandescence beneath some fallen leaves. He sank to the ground to uncover the shiftcrystal.

Clarin and Shay appeared over the treetops and flew at Illsworth, their mouths open to shoot. With everyone else safe within QuinKell, they had immediately set out to try to recover Phaed's hallowed—and potentially power-laden—shiftcrystal. From above, Illsworth's vultures intercepted the dragon parents. The devices the vultures bore were tripped by Illsworth to release the dragondregs of all four of their children's natures.

Clarin and Shay crashed to the ground, landing in a wasted heap. Illsworth gestured to his man ducking nearby. As the two villains approached the dragons, Illsworth rubbed his hands together greedily. "You grab the blue one," he shouted to his henchman, as he himself advanced on Clarin.

Flashing lights and sirens crashed through the brush a hundred yards away, interrupting the reprehensible poachers. Clarin and Shay regained consciousness enough to scratch at their would-be kidnappers as the deputy's SUV closed in. Illsworth reached to grab Clarin's neck, undeterred by the dragon's strengthening resistance that resulted in deep scratches on his arms and neck. His thug hesitated. "I said, *get him*," Illsworth commanded through clenched teeth. "I've got more dragondregs right here." As he reached into a front shirt pocket, Clarin began to glow with burgeoning firebreath. The SUV was bearing down as Shay now arched his wings and stabbed his sharp thumb talons into the shoulders of the man trying to subdue him.

"Leave them!" Illsworth shouted with enough bitterness to wilt the surrounding flora while pushing Clarin violently to the ground. He and his man ran away from the headlights and into the darkness. Clarin and Shay crawled under the nearest bushes and, though grateful, stole away from the officers who were now coming to a stop just a few yards from the struggle. Within minutes, the dragons' powers had recharged sufficiently for them to fly to the safe haven and rejoin their family.

Illsworth, out of sight of the officers who had foiled him and his helpmate, deposited the shiftcrystal in his pocket and disappeared toward the security of his grounds.

Chapter Twenty-Two

The Namings

The quiet blackness wrapped the dragon family in deepest peace. Eleven hatchlings slept on the soft dirt cave floor, their parents' bodies arched around them for this, their first night within the QuinKell, and their first night in the new lair of their dragonkin. The intermittent embers of their collective heartfires presented a faint, pulsing, but colorful light show.

Spread across the earthen shelf at the front of the cave, the eleven mistcrystals glowed and swirled—golden, crimson, azure, and pearl—each in unison with the originator who curled in serenity between the parents.

Tomorrow: the namings and the consecration of the lair would take place, a new beginning of the record of the dragonkin family tree.

Clarin awoke. Her mate's dazzling blue eyes found her across their family. Ayan slept in the far corner, the last place in the lair where the morning light would creep. Three firesavings Clarin had already performed, each bringing their son a little closer to himself. His regeneration would take days, maybe weeks. The darkness, the mineral synthesis between him and his father, and his mother's healing would restore his nature. The QuinKell would restore his faith.

The dragon family slept. In peace and complete darkness, save for their glowing heartfires, they slept.

Diana could not sleep. In her room, in her own house, within the harmonious vibrations of the QuinKell, her thoughts turned and turned. Her father. They would find him. They had the safe haven they needed to understand what Illsworth was up to. They would find her dad. In the meantime, eleven dragons would grow up and Ayan would be himself again and take his place among the dragonkin.

She had been texting Nicki and Jake and finally said goodnight. Tomorrow their lives could be lived semi-normally, whatever normal was now. But tomorrow Diana would also live in the magic of the namings and the mistcrystals. She lay back on her bed and pulled up the covers, holding her mistcrystal as its warm, steady pulse lulled her into slumber.

"Come on, wake up!" Brody jumped on the end of Diana's bed. She bolted to a seated position. "What time is it?" Before she even looked at her phone, she realized all was well. The mistcrystal remained evenly thrumming.

She got up, shut the door to the bathroom on her little brother's nose, came out with her toothbrush in her mouth, walked to her room— Brody still on her heels—shut the door to her bedroom, again on his nose, and grabbed her clothes from the drawers; she walked back to the bathroom with Brody trailing her, put her toothbrush away and ran back to her room, shutting her now frantic brother out again and locking the door.

"I wanna go with you. I wanna see the dragons!" Brody protested through the wood. No answer. He rapped repeatedly. "Come on, pleeeeeease..." he whined.

"Not today," his sister said through the closed door. "They have to be named. I wish I could take you, but—" Diana opened the door, her clothes thrown on sloppily, socks in hand, "but you need one of these," she held up her mistcrystal, "to be at the namings." Brody grabbed for the mistcrystal, not really trying since he was more than a little awed, if not slightly frightened, by the amulet. Diana sat on the stairs to tie her shoes, too impatient to tighten them properly and barely looping the short pieces of lacing. The formerly sparkling edges of the shoes were caked in dirt from the day before. It seemed like weeks ago.

Diana ran down the stairs and into the kitchen. "Breakfast!" her mother shouted from her office off the back hallway.

"Got it!" Diana said, then grabbed a whole bagel from the bag and chugged orange juice from the carton. Brody looked at her with a budding "I'm telling" look that he quickly abandoned in favor of chasing her through the room to the door. She ran out of the house with Brody following her to the edge of the grass, where he contemplated the effects of the coarse, wild desert terrain on his bare feet. Linda came to the back door and he walked back, sulking, when she called him inside.

The dew stuck to Diana's purple high-tops. She ran toward the hideaway—now the dragonkin lair—zig-zagging because of habit, not necessity. The birds seemed to sing louder, but really there were just so many more of them here, now.

Diana hopped the creek and rounded the boulder that marked the opening of the cave. A dragon family—her dragon family—lived here. She could not stop smiling. *Do I knock?* she thought, laughing at herself. Then she heard

Clarin's happy vocalization in her head, *Come, Diana. Come in.*

The scene she witnessed brought her to her knees, mostly because the excited dragonlings began to jump all over her. The whole cave was filled with motion, dragons hopping and trying to fly. It was like a dance of jewel-toned scarves in the wind, the colors moving around her feet and past her eyes where she now sat on the earth floor. The baby terra perched on the stool Diana kept in the cave. The little golden dragonling turned herself into smoky vapor and back again, time and again, a performance piece of "now-you-see-me; now-you-almost-don't." Diana laughed and thought, *You're quite a character.*

To her astonishment, the baby terra flew up close to her face and stared her down. Diana half expected to hear it say *Are you talking to me?* but the voice would appear only later today when the child received its name, and then, Diana reflected with a tinge of melancholy, only to the other dragons.

Diana got up, brushing playfully at a baby sun who would not let go, even though Diana's vertical positioning took the dragon two feet off the ground. It dropped and rolled around, knocking a couple of brothers and sisters, creating a frisky sibling brawl. Diana walked toward Clarin and Shay, who had reclaimed the perches where she had first found them. The parents watched the youngsters with tired and happy gazes. Next to them, in the darkest corner, Ayan slept. *How is he?* Diana inquired of Clarin.

He improves. He will feel himself to be our whole ghost son soon. Clarin and Shay looked to their sleeping dragon child. *During the namings, Diana, please stay with him.* Diana nodded. *He is not yet well, and we must guard against anything troubling him,* Clarin finished.

Diana went to the mistcrystals and watched their brilliancies wax and wane in the mist and color contained there: *their first fire breaths.* She ran her hand back and forth just above the array, feeling the warmth and watching the light reflect on her palm. She reached to her throat. The magnitude of the gift she wore filled her.

Ayan awoke. Shay floated to him and began another round of mineral synthesis. Ayan's breath brightened and his scales took on a healthier luster. His young siblings crept toward their father and big brother dragon. No impression of the Ayan who had been under

Illsworth's manipulations lingered in the baby dragons. They wanted to play. But even the new and unnamed sensed that it was not yet time.

Clarin beckoned to Diana as Shay led Ayan to sit next to his humankin sister, off to the side of the lair entrance. Ayan was still much cooler than the other grown dragons, but his subtle warmth floated gently over the air to tap Diana's shoulder. She took a deep breath and let out a sigh.

The sun reached its apex. Clarin and Shay called their children to them, with intent, not words. The dragonlings ceased their antics and lined up to face their parents. Before naming their new children, Diana heard Clarin—Shay, too, she gathered by the look on his face—think the name of their lost child: *Phaed*. The children awaiting names stood motionless, all eyes on their parents. Clarin and Shay turned to the stone wall at the head of the cave. Each blew a tiny burst of fire onto the same spot, first Shay, then Clarin. The resulting mark was a pearly symbol. Everyone whispered in thought, *Phaed*. Then they let him go, vowing to one another to recover his shiftcrystal, as well as that of the unknown perished dragon egg, misbegotten in the hands of Marcurius Illsworth.

Clarin and Shay turned back to their living family. Behind the mother and father, the first-hatched dragonling's mistcrystal began to whir. A twinkling seascape churned within the hammered gem, beckoning the dragonling to pass through the narrow space between its parents and flutter on tentative wings toward it. Clarin and Shay turned inward and leaned toward their dragon child. Clarin effused firefog and Shay firemist, together creating a celestial curtain, parted by the first child—a sea—whose scales glowed iridescent aqua. The dragonling blew a tiny halo of azure fire that settled over its mistcrystal. The ring of fire rose, lifting and floating the mistcrystal through the air. It drifted to its dragonling and touched the center of its forehead, bouncing off and surging away from the dragon, the energy and momentum pulling the dragonling forward nearly prostrate. The baby sea righted itself in time to watch its mistcrystal fuse slowly and deliberately into the rock of the cave wall. As the consecrating fire went out, the baby and its parents shared, in one unified thought, its name:

Khero.

The baby fluttered back to its parents, receiving the *naming kiss* from each: first by the father, then the mother, on the shining place on its forehead its mistcrystal had just touched.

A baby sun came forward. It passed through the soft gauntlet of haze to inflame its red-orange gem. The mistcrystal floated to perform the naming touch, then embedded itself permanently in the wall. Then the family, including the first-named sibling, all heard her name:

Raya.

Next came a sun son:

Xarien.

Then two sun daughters:

Sahvi.

Fabel.

The little terra came forward on sure wings, gliding through the gentle, parental mist. As its mistcrystal rose in an amber corona, the dragon bowed, rather than fell, after the naming kell touch. Her mistcrystal fused in the family wall, and they all heard the new terra's name:

Si'la.

She accepted the kiss from her parents. Before settling with the others now named, she floated softly to Diana and touched her forehead to that of the human sister.

The ghost hatchling parted the cloudy way to the front, his alabaster scales nearly lost in the mist. As the naming kell ended, his family welcomed him, the ghost hatchling who survived:

Ethari.

Then came two sea sons:

G'zyn.

No'ri.

And a sea daughter:

Migo.

The last sun son received the final name:

Sehsi.

The ritual concluded. The parents filled the cavern with a last billow of haze while the dragonlings practiced saying and hearing their names, and chased the billowing fog like a human toddler chasing bubbles. Ayan stood and parted the way, meeting his parents in the center. The newly named siblings ran up to Ayan, who, with his baby brother ghost clambering to perch on his wing, received the brood with the reserve his healing body required, not what his healing heart desired.

Diana carefully waded her way to Clarin. *The names are incredible.* Diana had heard each name as it floated from Clarin's mind. Diana now felt she was floating.

Thank you, dear Diana.

May I get the others? She bounced on the balls of her feet. Diana had been in something of a trance, and now she felt like she'd just heard the last school bell before summer.

Of course, answered Clarin, smiling at Diana with her eyes.

Diana ran to the house and scaled the back stairs in two huge leaps, shouting to Brody. She had to call Jake and Nicki from the land-line because of the interference of the frequencies of the QuinKell.

While his big sister made the calls, Brody chomped at the bit. As soon as she hung up, he started to ask a hundred questions. Diana merely laughed. "Just come on!" Her mother was right behind them. They ran to the cave to see the dragonlings spilling out of it. Diana tried to point them out, but they moved so quickly she could hardly convey the names. Brody chased them like he chased birds on the beach, and they chased him back.

In fifteen minutes, Dr. Kim, Jake, Sheriff Gonzales, and Nicki arrived, bringing another avalanche of questions and joy. Nicki sat on the boulder and tried to memorize the names she had gathered, letting the dragonlings hop up on her shoulders and knees. Jake went in and checked out Ayan, sorry for what he'd had to do the day before, but seeing that the dragon was in much better shape. He watched for a while as the son received more rejuvenation from his father, then was happy to run out and join the festive scene. He put a name to a dragon or two, got them wrong, switched them around again and laughed. "I'll just have a favorite and learn that one."

Dr. Kim smiled at that and ducked as the little ghost, Ethari, flew toward her and nearly hit her in the head. He wobbled and she caught him on the way down. "You'll get it," she chuckled, setting the transparent little guy down on a rock. Linda kept her eyes on Brody, though there was not much need. It seemed he had finally met his matches.

The little terra, Si'la, flew deftly between Diana and Clarin, banking around her mother and flying back into the cave, straight through the center of the circular entry. A moment later, she flew back out and gained more height.

That gives me an idea, Diana teasingly thought to the mother dragon beside her. Clarin's eyes smiled, and with a thought she asked her mate to come out to supervise their brood. Shay came to the cave entrance, Ayan by his side.

Clarin reached into the loose soil outside their home and cast Diana's elementor onto widening talons. Once the delicate wings had coalesced onto Diana's frame, the two took off, soaring above the cave, the fields, the trees, and Diana's house.

308

"I don't suppose I'll ever get used to that," Linda Santos said, smiling, not bothering to be loud enough to be heard.

Diana and Clarin soared over the canyons. The sun danced on the dragon's golden scales, and lit up Diana's elementor and the highlights in her hair. They circled the topmost reach of the QuinKell, a shimmering tent a hundred stories high.

Look! Diana thought, pointing to the eastern edge of the phenomenon. Clarin followed Diana's gesture, unsurprised but delighted, while Diana wondered at the sight. Where the creek exited the QuinKell, along the otherwise dull, everyday browns and muted greens of the desert scrub, a few feet of bright green stems, leaves, and budding flowers sprung up around the water.

~

Outside the boundary, Illsworth stood in his manor. He glared out onto the desert land, seeing the dragon and girl flying carefree. On his hand, the red shiftcrystal mounted in silver seemed to twitch, an irregular flicker occurring in the black fracture through the center. He held the newly stolen artifact, Phaed's shiftcrystal, its cracked, red core also beating like a heart attack within the milky white gem. Behind Illsworth, vessels of faded dragondregs lined the far wall, and the vultures cried for their dinner.

~

Diana and Clarin soared on, each taking turns leading the way, careful to stay within the soft ambiance of the QuinKell. *Is it just me—?* Diana thought to Clarin, pointing to a small cluster of oak saplings where the stream exited the magical milieu. Clarin finished Diana's thought: *It's not just you, Diana. I see it, too. Yes—the trees are already greener.*

The End

Book Two Coming Soon!

Diana's Dragons
The Stolen

By J.R. Schumaker

(Vignette)

The Captive

The corner of the cave where Jeff Santos found himself was bare and shallow. And it was guarded by vultures.

It was not that he couldn't leave the tiny alcove, but should he wander a few feet toward the main chamber, the birds were upon him, and not just with their natural arsenal. Had beaks and talons been the only threats, he would have run for it long ago. No, around each bird's neck was a rectangular medallion bearing the ouroboros–the symbol that Clarin had fused into the puzzle box. And whatever those devices were, they gave the screeches of those vultures the power to lay Jeff Santos flat.

The pain was nearly unbearable; the paralysis was insurmountable.

Jeff had tried running twice. The first time, the vultures didn't move until he was a few yards past them. Then in unison, they attacked. At his head and arms their talons scratched, but this lasted only a few seconds and was the least of the onslaught.

Their screeches—the noise pounded his skull. He felt like the asphalt under a jackhammer. He fell to the ground and twitched helplessly in the black dirt as the painful distortions swept through him. Once the vibrations in his head wore off, it was several minutes before the use of his muscles returned. He lay on the floor of the forest clearing and watched the creatures circle, as he waited for even the tiniest movement of his pinky to respond to his brain's desperate command: *move.*

The second time he tried it, everything doubled in intensity and duration. He knew he would not survive a third attempt.

The dragon-poaching lunatic who kept him here had forced him from the large, center chamber of the dragonkin's ancestral lair—the lair viciously hijacked from Clarin and Shay. Jeff Santos had dwelled among the recessed black walls and dragon pellets since he'd been caught digging around and stockpiling dragon scales.

It was too bad, too, for the obvious reason that it robbed Santos of any shred of new observations on the madman's schemes. It also robbed him of one of the things that had helped keep him going: the cave walls embedded with thousands of living mistcrystals. The sparkling stones seemed to whisper to him with all the first breaths of the dragonkin. For countless generations, each and every mistcrystal became a permanent part of the dragonkin's lair, the abstract birth record of every dragon ever born to them, including Clarin and Shay and their first brood. The effect was a dazzling, breathing kaleidoscope. When the morning light spilled in, the reflections danced in a million prismatic rainbows all around him.

Even the scrap of sunlight that made it through to the dismal inner chamber was enough to set off a show of light. During those times, he got the strangest feeling that he'd known the dragon family all his life; that his grandparents had known their grandparents. Mr. Santos laughed aloud at himself. That would be a good trick: his grandfather knowing Clarin's, considering the fact that dragons lived about three times as long as humans. For all the horror of being entrapped there, Jeff Santos could not help but wish his family could have seen what he saw, especially Diana, his little honorary dragon.

Of course, he had to remind himself many times that Diana was not such a little girl anymore. She was twelve now. Twelve: he could barely comprehend it. And Brody was seven. The realization hit him hard, just as it did every time he calculated the months—now years—since their last two birthdays, two new school years, two summers he and Linda would have worked while Diana and Brody played, until a crazy last-minute vacation they would cook up overnight and spring on the kids.

Linda. How he missed her. He still reached for her in the night, to be awakened by pangs of loss that felt brand new every time. How was she coping with his absence? The not knowing? She was left to raise their kids without him while they all lived in the uncertainty. There was no one stronger for it, he knew; and Diana was a strong, smart girl who'd be there for her mom and little Brody. Jeff winced inside, feeling like his heart was folding in on itself with the ache of missing those who lived there.

Jeff had done all he could to get a warning back to them. He wasn't sure of his jailer's plot. Even when he'd managed to send the message box back with Clarin and Shay, he hadn't had much of the half-information he now possessed. He had to hope that Diana and the dragons could put it all together: that Illsworth was hardly their biggest threat; that the dragons were in terrible danger; that he both needed them desperately and desperately wanted to help them.

This maniac who imprisoned Jeff could count on Marcurius Illsworth for only so much. Jeff Santos was still alive for one reason: his captor needed the dragons to come for him. At some point, everything would come back to the rainforest.

~

Please visit dianasdragons.com to find out more about the second book in the *Diana's Dragons* quadrilogy:
Diana's Dragons: The Stolen

About the author...

J.R. Schumaker has a Bachelor of Arts in theology with minors in philosophy and French from Creighton University in Omaha, Nebraska. She also attended College of Saint Mary, completing the program in elementary education with an emphasis on adolescent literature. She is a former freelance writer, editor, newspaper columnist, and contributor to many blogs, online magazines, and websites.

Diana's Dragons: The Awaited began as a bedtime story Schumaker made up for her four children in 2001. Once the children were asleep, the author ran down the hall to her computer and wrote out the highlights of the story. After a long sleep in the hard drive while the children grew up, the magical creatures stirred restlessly, so Schumaker refilled her nest with four natures of dragons and our hero, Diana.

Diana's Dragons: The Awaited is the first book in a quadrilogy. Apparently, the author likes the number four.

J.R. Schumaker is the single mother of three sons and a daughter, now adults. Her oldest son is the father of her first, quite magical, grandchild.

J.R. Schumaker works from home—and from various coffee shops—in San Diego County, California.

316

Heartfelt thanks to my many supporters:

My parents: John R. Schumaker, PhD: proud, loving dad and head cowboy; and Vera S. (Hurst) Schumaker: proud, loving mom and head proofreader. My beloved sister, Lisa Schumaker: world's best sis and brilliant developmental editing consultant a-go-go. My brother, Jeffrey Russell Schumaker, May 23, 1964 - September 20, 1995, may he rest in peace.

Joshua-Jose Schumaker Bello, Miguel Russell Schumaker Bello, Olivia Raquel Schumaker Bello; Noah Rafael Schumaker Bello and Brianna Puckett (daughter-in-law to be, daughter-in-heart, already) and Rachel Maya Bello (granddaughter, princess, spitfire, and future pediatric brain surgeon).

Franc Uberti, whose music inspired me, gourmet food nourished me, perfect coffee kept me going, and who believed in me all the way.

Mauri Shayegi Ashley (I told you when we were 10, I was going to be your friend); Karen Avossa, Delaney B., Carter B., Alice Bandy (to whom I'm eternally grateful), Carrie Bastian.

Brian Bielawski, Ken Bien, Stephen Boe, Paul Boisvert and Rick Marshall (like brothers to me),

Boise Unitarian Universalist Fellowship; Becky and Carolyn Bolton. Angelina Camacho and Renate Schumaker, Jaclyn Cannon.
Chalice Unitarian Universalist Congregation, Alicia Champion and Danielle LoPresti and son, Lucian; Clare and Angie, Lori Cleary, Richard Conviser, Tierney Coughlin.

Connie Gawryluk and her angel, Jacob "Jake" Clair Brummer.

Creighton University, Delaney and Roman, Nia DeShon, Charles (Tim) Dickel, PhD; John DiGiovanni, Angie Dilliard, Jerry Dilliard, Max DisPosti (fratello e caro), Victoria Do (graphic arts intern), Sue Doyle (in memory of niece Taylor Gettinger); John Evangelista, Amy Fan, Suzanne Fitzmaurice, OSB; Mary Forte, Matthew Fuller.

Robert Gleason, Yael Gmach, Dean Goddette, Paula Gonzales (embodiment of generosity of heart), Diane Griffitts, Linda Griffitts (web designer, writing retreat host, and "fruity red" supplier). Peter H., Deb Hall, Kerriee Hall, Michael Hampson (digital marketing consultant and honorary uncle to my brood); Sandra Hapenney, Holly Harper, Robyn Harper.

Wendy Harrison, Gail Hawkins, Luke Henderson, Sandra Herrera, Nicole Holloway (Cuzzo "Nicky"!), Peter and Dianne Houser, Valerie Reeves Hoynes and Brendan Hoynes; Glenn Hurst and Rhonda Noel-Hurst; Tom Interval, Blaise and Theresa Jackson.

Rev. Beth Johnson (God-mother to our animal family); Avery Katz, Saroj Khanal, Mike Kirkeby, Briana Kosmicki, and Debbie Kosmicki and Greg Kosmicki (poet and publisher); Davina Kotulski, Michael G. Lawler, PhD; Richard Lederer (renowned author, speaker, radio host, and more).

Mark Leno, Shana Lew, Danny and Peggy Litwhiler, Fernando Zweifach Lopez, Jr. (love warrior).Karina Lopinto y su angel, Daiana Ayelen Garcia.Dustin Lundberg, Katie Mansfield, Grace M. Martinez, Antoinette and Stuart Matlins, Lesa Bird McConnel.

Ernie McCray. Diana Shenefelt McHenry, Anne McKeirnan, Michele and Bryan McMeekin, Cindy Lee Meier, Emmett Meier, Elissa Mendenhall and Gracella, Walter G. Meyer, (writer, speaker, and author of *Rounding Third*); Romel Monzon.Ruth Moore, Sophia Morales, The Muglia Family: Wendy, Scott, Dakota, Dylan, and Colton (love you 4 life, too).

Bob and Dale Muldrow, Janet Myers, Jessica M-E Nitsch, Ha Nguyen, Betty Owen, Deborah Morton, Meredith O'Gwynn, Laura Payne, Aeryn Pecha, John Pecha, Keith and Brook Pecha, Joseph

Phillips, PhD.Laura Preble, Mary Pryde, Robin Rice, Jim Rogers.

Lauren Ruggles (Copy Editor); Dr. Jane Russell, OSF; The Scales Family: Kaarina, Michael, Natalie, Liam, and Tiffany; Kai Schierwater, Drs. Jeanne Schuler and Patrick Murray (writing retreat hosts and dear friends and mentors).

Dr. David Schultenover, SJ; Kirstin Schumaker, Oren and Michelle Schumaker, Hannah Scroggins, Patrick Sherman, The Spoto Family, Ann Sexton Stephens, Andi and Bill Stout, Dan Swart, John Swart, Joseph Swart, Jen Taylor, "La" Tessieri. Bill and KK Uberti, Margo Uhl (writing retreat host and dear pal since C.U. days).

Jim and Jamie Ulrich, Delaney Valenzuela, Neal and Pam Washburn, Marie Watson, Antonio Wellman, Lena Wellman, Pattie Wells, Al Weiss, Roger and Mary Ann Wilcox, Janet F. Williams, Natalie Wilson, Wout Wynants, Jamie Leno Zimron.

Made in the USA
San Bernardino, CA
10 April 2020

67423837R00200